WITHDRAWN FROM
KENT STATE UNIVERSITY LIBRARIES

HOPE'S HIGHWAY
A Novel

AMS PRESS
NEW YORK

HOPE'S HIGHWAY

A Novel

BY

SARAH LEE BROWN FLEMING

THE NEALE PUBLISHING COMPANY
440 FOURTH AVENUE, NEW YORK
MCMXVIII

Library of Congress Cataloging in Publication Data

Fleming, Sarah Lee Brown
   Hope's highway.

   I. Title.
PZ3.F6295Ho10   [PS3511.L445]   813'.5'2   76-144607
ISBN 0-404-00158-0

Trim size of original edition: 4 7/8 X 7 5/16"
Trim size of AMS edition: 5 X 6 7/8"

From the edition of 1918, New York
First AMS edition published in 1973
Manufactured in the United States of America

AMS PRESS INC.
NEW YORK, N.Y. 10003

TO

THE FOLLOWING LEADERS, LIVING AND DEAD, WHO
HAVE CHAMPIONED, AND STILL CHAMPION, THE
HIGHER ASPIRATIONS OF THE BLACK MAN

THIS BOOK IS DEDICATED

HON. FREDERICK DOUGLASS
HON. GEORGE T. DOWNING
HON. ROBERT B. ELLIOTT
HON. RICHARD T. GREENER
HON. WRIGHT CUNEY
HON. FRANK GRIMKE
HON. ARCHIBALD H. GRIMKE
HON. JOHN M. LANGSTON
HON. EBENEZER D. BASSETT
JUDGE JOSEPH LEE
DR. BOOKER T. WASHINGTON
DR. W. E. BURGHARDT DU BOIS
BISHOP A. WALTERS

TABLE OF CONTENTS

		PAGE
Foreword		9

CHAPTER		PAGE
I.	Santa Maria	11
II.	John Vance	16
III.	Grace Ennery	22
IV.	The Leader's Funeral	29
V.	The Lynching	35
VI.	Santa Maria, Past and Present	43
VII.	Grace Ennery's Return to New York	50
VIII.	The Letter That Failed	57
IX.	The Proposal	63
X.	Fred Trower in the South	73
XI.	The Farmers' Conference	80
XII.	Tom Brinley in Chains	85
XIII.	Tom Brinley's Escape to the North	89
XIV.	Tom in Love	99
XV.	Tom Brinley Rescues Grace Ennery	106
XVI.	Spirited Away	114
XVII.	The Wedding	123
XVIII.	The Trial	129
XIX.	Tom Brinley at Oxford	138
XX.	The Call of His People	149

FOREWORD

I have gained much information regarding the achievements and political status of the black man in America, and beyond the seas, from "The African Abroad," by William H. Ferris, A. M.

S. L. B. F.

HOPE'S HIGHWAY

CHAPTER I

SANTA MARIA

Beautiful Santa Maria, land of the gods that nestles beneath wondrously blue skies, lies upon a luxurious carpet of green, on a prominence overlooking,—as did Psyche of the myths in her liquid mirror of old,—the limpid Bay of Joan.

In the seventeenth century wealthy Spaniards had come over here in large numbers from the Old World and, because of its seclusion, had chosen this heavenly spot for a home. Across the bay was to be seen another ideal place, Santa Barbara, where to-day only the ruins of a once most extensive cotton plantation remain to show the existence of former grandeur. Negro men and women may be seen working in the fields, which show a few patches of cultivation. Rickety cabins, scattered thickly here and there, tell the tale of the passing of the masters of this once thriving island and of the reign of the Blacks; for investigation will show that no white man lives there now.

In Santa Maria may also be seen ruins of an old monastery, built by the Spaniards in the seventeenth century. After the state became a part of the Union, and the Spaniards gradually dispersed, other settlers came to this secluded spot, which, until the Emancipation, was one of the most aristocratic plantation settlements of the whole South. And in those days cabin life of the better sort was a conspicuous feature of beautiful Santa Maria and of its neighbor, Santa Barbara. It seemed the purpose of the owners of the Blacks to have this the one place where slavery was of a higher order,—if degrees of serfdom be possible.

The approach to Santa Maria was very beautiful. Imagine a shell-road of great length and width, lined on either side with drooping willows,—moss-laden,—some interlocking, forming spacious arches, and others opening sufficiently at the top to let in the Southern sunlight in all its regal splendor. The effect was almost fairylike. And to add enchantment to the scene, one could for an instant imagine these drooping willows bowing, as it were, most hospitably to the traveler, as if ushering him on and on to the resplendent glories of Santa Maria.

In the days of its glory,—after the traveler had left the willows behind,—imposing residences might be seen as far as the eye could reach.

From the quarters, on summer nights, plantation melodies were wafted on balmy breezes, and, as one drew nearer, crooning lullabies, sung by dusky mothers, could be heard,—lullabies so full of rest and hope.

Honey, take yo' res, on yo' mamme's breas',
See dat light,—a-fadin' 'mong de pine trees in de wes',
Yes; de day is gone, night is comin' on,
Darksome night mus' come to us befo' another dawn.

Whippo'will is callin',—callin' to his mate;
Mockin'-bird is callin', too;
Pine trees is a-sighin', babies is a-cryin',
As de darksome night is passin' through.
Go to sleep, ma little baby, go to sleep;
Shut yo' weary eyelids, an' don' you weep;
Sleep an' take yo' res', on yo' mamme's breas',
Night can never harm you here.

Honey, don' you see, dat it's got to be:
Day an' night, yes, day an' night, till yo' spirit's free;
Den you'll quit ma breas' fur to go an' res'
Wid another who can keep you safe from harm de bes'.

Masters here were more or less kind to their slaves, and, consequently, their reputation for gentleness spread far and wide. At the slave market one might observe a striking evidence of this; for whenever a buyer from Santa Maria or Santa Barbara came along, every slave showed up at his best upon the auction block.

When the deathknell to slavery was sounded and Lincoln signed the great Emancipation

Proclamation,—which spelled Liberty for millions of slaves,—a great many of the Blacks in Santa Maria and Santa Barbara remained with their owners.

Of these slaveholders, John Vance,—regarded as one of the wealthiest in this realm,— freed and educated one of his loyal servitors, with the idea that, should the freedom that the bondmen craved come to them, he could impart to his people some of the essentials necessary for a recently emancipated race to understand. Thus, Enoch Vance, taking his master's name, attracted much attention by his application and brilliancy at a Western university and returned to his former owner at the announcement of Freedom. Fortunately, he arrived in Santa Maria a few months before his benefactor's death.

John Vance, because of the manumission of the Negroes, had lost some of his vast fortune, but in his great generosity, he left nearly half of what was left for the education of the Blacks, whom slavery had kept so long in ignorance.

Upon his deathbed he sent for his former slave.

"Go," said he to Enoch, "and upon the land I shall give you, at the entrance of this beautiful Santa Maria,—land that I love so well,— facing the drooping willows and the shell-road,

SANTA MARIA 15

erect a school that shall be a guiding star to your people, lost on the road of ignorance. Be a leader to them,—be a Moses,—safely carrying them over the Red Sea to the Promised Land!"

CHAPTER II

JOHN VANCE

John Vance's name was held in reverence by every Negro in and around Santa Maria. How many Black men and women in slavery had heard of this good man and prayed that some day they might become his property! Often, on moonlight nights, he would listen to the singing of his slaves, as they sat in their cabin doors, voicing the familiar plantation melodies,—the effect of which was marvelous,—as it passed from door to door on the balmy breezes. One song that particularly pleased their master was:

Lord, I'd rather go to Glory, Lord, I'd rather go to Glory,
Lord, I'd rather go to Glory, than to leave this master kind.

John Vance was in the habit of visiting his slaves in their cabins, he would talk with them, and thus he became a part of their lives. He never had occasion to whip a slave, never kept an overseer, neither did he ever have a runaway. When a slave became in any way obstinate or unruly, the master would only have to suggest in a kindly way, that perhaps the bondman would like another master; and, almost invariably, he would get the result he desired. He could count upon the fingers of one hand,—out of a thousand or more slaves that he owned,—the few cases he could not handle.

Being of a very sympathetic nature, he often wanted to help many a one who yearned for an education; for if there was any aristocrat in the South who desired to change the existing laws regarding educating slaves, John Vance truly was one. As soon as freedom came, he secured teachers for those of the adults that desired to learn, while the children were compelled to spend a certain number of hours each day in the schoolroom. Indeed, his was the first institute for Blacks in the South, being the forerunner of the many organizations that were established for this race by loyal Northern supporters.

The young Negro lad, Enoch, whom John Vance specially favored, was born upon the Vance plantation, as was his mother. His father had been bought by Vance from a neighboring slaveholder,—who had lost heavily in speculation. The father of Enoch had courted and married Enoch's mother; and when the son was born his mother felt that the boy was destined to be a Moses to his people.

Knowing how Enoch's mother yearned for an

education, and seeing the same desire manifested by the lad, John Vance hoped that he might be able to start him on the road of knowledge. He was fortunately able to do this, by giving the lad his freedom and sending him to that greatest of Western colleges, which has ever held and which still holds open the "Door of Hope" to all who would enter therein. Thus Enoch developed into a true leader of his people, for he was the first Negro qualified to teach the Blacks in the South after Emancipation.

When John Vance lay dead in the Big House, Negroes came from far and near to view the abode of this true lover of humanity. Many, too poor to buy flowers, wrought wreaths out of wild flowers and lay them at the entrance of the Big House. Children could be seen strewing flowers in the familiar spots and along the roads he frequented. Men and women wept like babies, as from their cabins they saw the body of their dearest friend borne to its final resting-place.

After the closing up of the Big House, the late owner's widowed sister, who had made her home with him, returned North to her husband's people. The division of his lands was made according to John Vance's dying wish, which gave his belongings to the ex-slaves that had served him faithfully. And these same people, by their frugality, became the hope of the South, while by their efforts great business enterprises were launched,—enterprises that to-day, together with the Institute, are the pride of the Black South.

This institute was a haven for the Negro. Located picturesquely at the entrance of Santa Maria and overlooking the Bay of Joan, it seemed almost a temple in a land of promise, and, flocking to its doors, came from all parts of the world, those eager to learn.

Enoch first made the curriculum cover those things that his people most needed,—agriculture and manual training; for he was aware that a people just emerging from slavery could need nothing more than the rudiments of education. As time advanced, however, other departments were added, and finally from the Leader's school emerged men and women fitted for every vocation in life.

The Leader was heralded far and wide for his great achievements. Even abroad he was talked of, and educators of distant lands visited his institute, for the purpose of studying his methods of instruction. Great men from different parts of the country either gave their support financially or otherwise to the Vance Institute, and from its example other schools sprang up, heralding, as did their Alma Mater, "Higher education for the Black man."

This system of enlightenment in the course of time became unpopular with a certain element in the South,—an element that crowded in after slavery from the mountainous districts to the west of Santa Maria, or that came in by immigration. And, as the slaveholding aristocracy passed out by death or migration, these people became leading figures, soon wielding the political ax that chopped down all things that were unfavorable to them,—among them, the political status of the Negro, whom they considered to be growing too powerful. Throughout the South, state after state disfranchised the Blacks and decreed against higher education for them. Thus, because of legislative interference, the great ambition of the Leader's life was blighted.

Joe Vardam, an enemy to the cause of the Blacks, worked his way forward politically, fighting with tooth and nail to have the whole educational curriculum changed, so far as higher education for Blacks was concerned.

Realizing that he was utterly powerless to contend with this powerful demagogue, the Leader was compelled to bend to his will and strike out from his course of study psychology, sociology, comparative literature, law, theology, mathematics, and the classics.

"We don't want any Niggers reading Latin and Greek," Joe Vardam would say. "Soon

JOHN VANCE

they'll be wantin' to call on us and be askin' to marry our daughters.''

The Leader remembered that his former master had often been upbraided in the State Conventions by this fellow, and he remembered, too, that Vardam had once shaken his fist in John Vance's face, remarking:

"If I ever get a chance to deal a blow at these damned Blacks, I'll deal some blow; believe me!"

True to his oath he dealt a deadly blow, and the Leader, hurt to the soul,—having had all his fond hopes blighted, and being powerless to ask, in the name of the law, protection in the exercise of a right that he considered sacred,—died of a broken heart, in the very prime of his manhood, leaving to the world the memory of a well-spent life.

CHAPTER III

GRACE ENNERY

PHILLIP ENNERY, a boyhood chum of John Vance's, was one of the great plantation owners in the prosperous days of Santa Maria. Phillip had two sons, one of whom, Francis, at his mother's death, left the South, when still a young man, with his share of the Ennery fortune, and entered the brokerage business in New York City. In the course of time he met a beautiful young woman, of Boston's most exclusive circle, and married her. She did not live long after the birth of her daughter Grace, and Francis Ennery was left a widower in New York with a little daughter of five years to look after.

Grace's maternal grandmother, who lived in Boston, was an invalid, and her uncle John Ennery had never married; thus the dear little girl, for a time after her mother's death, was dependent upon strangers. This fact was a source of some worry to her grandmother, who realized that, unless she could arrange to have the child under her guidance,—even though she were disabled, that the little girl would be brought up among paid attendants. This she felt would not be the best thing for a child so young. Thus a plan was adopted by which Grace could remain with her grandmother until she should be old enough to enter a boarding school. After a competent governess had been secured, Francis Ennery returned from the "hub" to New York, grieved that his happy home life should be thus shattered.

Grace's grandmother was of Puritan stock, and reverenced those ideals for which her forefathers, desiring to enjoy freedom in a new land, had braved the dangers of the ocean and the terrors of warlike tribes. This love for liberty was so early implanted in the child's mind that we find her eager to hear the great stories of struggle and sacrifice and privation, for freedom's sake,—stories that her grandmother took pride in telling her.

As she sat with her grandmother she learned of the historical interest associated with the many places in and around Boston; and when she went out for her daily walks, she beheld these spots and loved them because of their glorious associations.

"Granny," she would often say, "tell me of the Boston Tea Party."

Then her grandmother would weave one of the prettiest tales concerning the "Tax on Tea."

Much enthused was she when she was told of the Battle of Bunker Hill, and how her great-great-grandfather had died in defense of the rights of the colonists and how her grandfather defended the rights of the slaves, taking an active part in the working of the famous "Underground Railroad." The story of how he helped them escape from their cruel masters in the South greatly interested her young mind.

Grace never grew weary of listening to the sorrows of the Blacks, and ofttimes she would say to Charlotte, her governess:

"Take me where I may see these people that Grandpa helped to get away from their bad masters. And, Charlotte, show me a man like Uncle Tom who was so good to little Eva."

As Grace grew to womanhood, she never forgot these pictures that her grandmother painted for her in such glowing colors. The Negro, wherever she met him, felt the sympathetic spirit for his sufferings that animated the girl.

The years flew rapidly by, and with them Grace grew, of course. Francis Ennery often came to see his daughter, who began to look more and more like her dead mother each day. At the suggestion of her grandmother, who was gradually declining, the father decided to send the child to a select boarding-school, as she was now twelve years of age. The day Grace bade her dear grandmother good-by was

GRACE ENNERY

a sad one for her. How she hated to leave this place, with all its dear associations; for it was her mother's birthplace, the storehouse of everything sacred in her child-mind. Then, too, she loved the implements of war,—relics of the family's bravery,—that had their places here and there around the house, from cellar to attic.

Her spirits were revived only when her grandmother told her that she was going to the same school from which her mother had been graduated. This, of course, pleased Grace in a way; but it did not prevent her crying herself to sleep for the first few nights after her entrance. However, the beauty of the scenery, her joy in her studies, the happiness of her teachers, and the spirited life of the school soon revived her youthful spirits.

Thus passed Grace Ennery's years from girlhood to womanhood, surrounded by every luxury; for she was a rich girl, yet poor, too, in that she was bereft of that richest of blessings, a fond mother, to whom she might now and again unburden herself,—one whom she might kiss and fondle with the abandon of a spoilt child. So, after all, Grace Ennery might be called a "Poor Little Rich Girl." Think of the loneliness that came to her young life at times! Think of the yearnings! "She had a father," you say. Yes, she did, and a devoted one, too; but he never filled that void, or satisfied an instinct that lay hidden within her soul. And because of her warmth of feeling and her passionate yearnings, it was a wonder that the suppression of her longing did not make her sad and pensive, and thus embitter her youthful existence. Grace, however, possessed an indomitable will, coupled with a courageous heart, which kept her from ever wincing. Hence there bloomed into womanhood, under the faithful guidance of the teachers of Saint Agnes school at Lynhurst, a girl who developed the most beautiful character,—noble, strong, and modest.

After her graduation, Grace was sent abroad to study art,—for which she had formed a decided talent,—chaperoned by one of her instructors, who also desired to make further studies in the same field. Miss Arnold, who was very much attached to Grace, made a pleasant traveling companion, and two delightful years were spent studying the old masters in the different countries of Europe.

One morning a most unexpected thing happened,—Grace received a cablegram announcing that her father had been advised by his physician to drop his business cares and responsibilities for the present and take a trip around the world, and that he wished to see her before sailing for the Orient, by way of the Mediterranean.

GRACE ENNERY 27

On Grace's receiving this news, Miss Arnold comforted her and assisted her in every possible way so that nothing might delay her departure. And Grace, after being placed in the care of good friends, was on her way to America.

She reached home just before her father sailed for Greece and Egypt. In one of his last talks with her he said:

"As I look upon your face, you so remind me of your dead mother, with your fluffy golden hair and large blue eyes. I pray that you may develop into the noble woman she was. Remember always, Grace, that you were her idol. I dislike to leave you at this time, when I know you should have me with you; but I must bow to my physician's command. You have an uncle in the South, in beautiful Santa Maria, where I was born. I hope upon my return from the East to gaze once more upon those moss-laden willows, under which I had my first boyish dreams.

"All alone in a great house he lives, upon a plantation where once your grandfather held numerous slaves. He writes that you must pay him a visit soon, when you will see one of nature's enchanting spots.

"I have made my home with the Grants for a number of years, and they have been very kind to me. If you do not return to your studies, make your home with them: I am sure they will be very good to you. The property and stocks left by your mother have been wisely invested and yield a large income. This, with other sums that I have placed in trust for you, will make it possible for you to grant your every wish while I am away. Deny yourself nothing, for there is plenty for everything.''

The next day Mr. Ennery left with his valet. Grace found herself pleasantly located in busy New York with her father's friends the Grants. After getting somewhat acquainted, she returned to her work in the world of art, where, because of her undoubted talent, she became quickly known. She found Mrs. Grant very busy with her numberless social duties,—entertaining and being entertained to a degree.

After a few months had elapsed, Grace decided to visit her uncle in Santa Maria. Shortly after her arrival, her uncle was called to Europe on business, and she was left in control of the place. She enjoyed the delights of the big house, but felt very lonely. So, wishing to see and learn a little more of the South, she took quarters in a nearby hotel.

Because of a deep sympathy for the Blacks, formed in her early years, it was her delight to wander with a friend or two,—but oftener alone, —in the neighborhoods where they were to be found, there to study their humble lives.

CHAPTER IV

THE LEADER'S FUNERAL

The Leader of his people lay dead, and as the funeral cortège wound its way into the peaceful graveyard, to lay at rest all that remained of a once powerful man, one could hear from the scattered groups of spectators such expressions as these:

"Who'll take his place?" "We'll now go to de dogs, for de white folks will surely do us bad." "Dey done peck on him an' peck on him till dey done kill him."

One of the old women began to sing, and others took up the strain:

> De Lord done take our Moses,
> De Lord done take our Moses,
> De Lord done take our Moses,—
> Who we gwine to follow now?

Deep into the heart of Tom Brinley sank these expressions; and, although but a boy of fifteen years, he was much disturbed. He suddenly felt the weight of a people upon his shoulders, and an irresistible impulse seized him to answer these poor dependent people.

30   HOPE'S HIGHWAY

Imagine a little brown boy,—bare-footed, with clothes covered with patches,—attempting to quell the sobbing multitude that had lost all hope, because of the death of the Leader! However, obeying the impulse, Tom sprang among the group of sobbing women, and with wide-open eyes,—eyes that brimmed over with sympathy,—and with the assurance of a man, cried out:

"Don't be sad; don't cry! Look at me. I'll lead you,—*I'll* be your Moses."

"O black boy,—with that look of exultation on your face,—surely some day you will be great with your wonderful determination. You truly have been sent to earth for some purpose. In your life the Divine will shine with such glorious brightness, that men will forget the hue of your skin!" thought Grace, who was present.

Surprised for an instant by Tom's words, the mourning groups temporarily forgot their grief and looked at the boy. When one woman had recovered sufficiently, she said:

"Go 'long, boy! You done gone stark crazy, you is."

Then a group of the rowdy element, of which the South is full, and who had gathered for no other purpose than curiosity, jeered at Tom, and one of them tripped him up. He fell against an iron rail, hitting his head, then lay upon the ground in a swoon.

THE LEADER'S FUNERAL 31

Some kind-hearted men picked him up and carried him to his home, which was not very far off. "What of his assailants?" you ask. This class compose the criminal element of the South. Many of the lynchings in that region are occasioned by the misdeeds of some one of this idle class of Negroes, who care little or nothing about leaders or rights. Then, too, the laws of the South had become so lax in the matter of offenses perpetrated by Blacks against Blacks that it was useless to complain.

Grace Ennery, who was a witness to all that had happened, followed the limp body of little Tom to his mother's cabin of two rooms.

Tom's mother was a quiet, sympathetic woman of about forty, with large, glowing eyes, and a slightly bent frame, which told of much drudgery.

"Tom truly has her eyes," thought Grace, as she looked upon the mother. When the men who carried Tom told of what had happened, her reply was:

"Tom's always bein' pecked on. Folks don' seem to understan' him."

Upon a clean but humble bed they placed the little lad. Grace Ennery assisted in bringing him to.

"I shall never forget his deep, soul-stirring eyes,—so full of purpose," she remarked to friends afterward. "As he came out of his swoon his first words were:

" 'All right, Hollow gang, you shall yet call me "Leader." Mother, didn't you hear our Leader say that when he was a little slave boy he would call the other slave children around him and tell them that he would some day be a great man and the leader of his people, and even they would not believe him?' "

"Yes," replied his mother, softly stroking his forehead.

"And, Mother," he continued, "see what a great man he became."

Grace Ennery listened to the little fellow with much interest, and when the crowd had somewhat disappeared, she asked the mother if she could be of any further service.

"Lor' bless you, dear lady," she replied. "Tom is given to dem fallin' out spells, whenever any one hits his head. When he use to work wid' Mister Joe, he would ofttimes send for me to ris' Tom out of dem spells, when he done hit him fur somethin'."

"Will you have those boys punished who willfully meddled with Tom?" asked Grace.

"Oh, Miss, you mus' be a stranger here?"

"Yes; I'm from the North."

"I thought so, ma'am. De white folks don' bother 'bout our troubles lessen they can't help it."

THE LEADER'S FUNERAL

"My! That is a very discouraging condition of affairs."

"Well, ma'am, we are gettin' so used to trouble, dat we don' look for justice till we die, an' then come judgment day," was the resigned reply.

Grace bade Tom good-by, and slipping a bill into his mother's hand, said:

"I expect to leave for the North in a few days, but will see you before I go."

Tom's mother bowed her visitor out graciously. It was somewhat new to her to have a sympathetic caller from the opposite race.

The Blacks at this time, owing to the injustice of Vardam, were so crushed that any white person having any relations with them other than those of employer and employed was considered an enemy to the cause of white supremacy. "Down with the Blacks!" was the slogan of Vardam and his allies.

Grace, of course, did not know of the sentiment regarding the Blacks, and even though she was the only white woman present, in her girlish optimism she had not observed it. Hers was a Divine sympathy, impartial and uncolored.

But, after all, a man's ideals, aspirations, hopes, and longings are not controlled by the color of his skin. Does not a brown horse that has broken his leg feel the same pain that a white horse does,—does he not demand the same amount of attention, regardless of the color of his hide?

CHAPTER V

THE LYNCHING

THE next day was Sunday, and after attending church, Grace had a strong desire to glance at the grave of the dead Leader. This desire had been interfered with on the previous day because of the accident to little Tom.

She had never seen the Leader, yet, even in the North, his fame had reached her ear and she had learned to respect him for his achievements among his people. His success was greatly appreciated by the North, and his advice had been sought by men of high as well as low degree.

Knowing all this, Grace was desirous of seeing the mound of dirt under which the body of this famed Negro rested. So she sauntered slowly to that spot on the grounds of the great school that he had established. She was not known, therefore was not interfered with. But one cross-looking white man, who, to Grace's mind, had the look of a man who might have been a cruel slaveholder (such as she had read about in "Uncle Tom's Cabin"), stopped her as she entered the grounds.

Turning around, Grace saw a picturesque but not a very prepossessing-looking individual, —a tall, raw-boned, and sinewy individual of about fifty, with a wide-brimmed slouch hat, tilted on one side; a long coat, and trousers tucked in leather boots, who walked with a long, swinging stride and spoke with a slow Southern drawl. But if his figure and attire were striking, his face was not attractive. Grace found herself looking into a pair of fierce devilish black eyes that gleamed beneath shaggy eyebrows. Besides these eyes she saw a decidedly hooked nose, which surmounted a thin, cruel mouth, and a long jaw, which was covered with a beard of medium growth.

But if the face was evil and sinister in repose, it took on added malignity as the man smiled sardonically. Plainly, here was a man with executive and administrative ability, with power to dominate the ignorant masses; a man possessed of a selfish, cruel nature.

"Say, miss," he said, "ain't you 'fraid to be travelin' in these Nigger haunts?"

"No," answered Grace, somewhat indignant. "So far you have been my only annoyance."

"Is that so?" was his surly query. "I guess you don't know who I am."

"Perhaps I don't, and neither do I care to know who you are, even if you were the governor."

THE LYNCHING 37

"Well, if you ever get into trouble with these Niggers, you needn't bother Joe Vardam," he retorted angrily, turning away.

Grace walked on and soon reached the Leader's grave. She had made no reply to Joe Vardam's last remark, neither had she looked back; but had kept on until she came to the spot that she was seeking. This she could not miss because of the profusion of flowers that covered it. She rested upon a stone coping and gazed upon the many-hued flowers that, in the sun's dancing rays, seemed to stir and send their mingled perfume up to Heaven.

While sitting there wondering about the people whom this worthy man represented, Grace was startled by a rustle of leaves behind her. It was the first of October, when nature clothed herself in gorgeous robes of crimson and gold, and even the ground was covered with a golden leafy carpet.

Her revery broken, she turned and saw Tom. As she looked up, he cried:

"Ain't de flowers pretty, missus? Look! de sun is comin' down to them."

And the boy stood there entranced by the wedding of the sun and the flowers.

"Tom, you loved your Leader?" asked Grace sympathetically.

"Yessum," answered Tom, still under the spell of the scene.

Grace continued:

"Did you go to his school?"

"Yessum," he replied again, still not taking his eyes away from the grave.

"He must have been a very wonderful man to impress you so strongly. I hope some day you will be as great and influential a man as he was."

"I will, ma'am, if Joe Vardam don't turn de hose on me as he did the Leader."

"Who is Joe Vardam?"

"Didn't you pass a man when you come in de school?"

"Yes, I remember that I did."

"Well, dat's de one, ma'am, who would kill us all up if he could. He's powerfully strong, missus."

"So he interfered with the progress of the school?"

"Yessum. Folks call him 'Goliath' here, and they is all 'fraid of him."

"I hope he may some day meet his David, Tom," retorted Grace with earnestness.

The chapel bell tolled two, and Grace arose to go, bidding Tom, who still was looking admiringly at the flowers, good-by. She told him that she would be leaving for her Northern home soon, but would see both him and his mother before she left.

THE LYNCHING

Grace walked slowly to her hotel, thinking of the sorrows of this race.

"O black boy," thought she, "too sensitive were you made! You, too, shall have many sorrows, for my people do not believe in 'Souls of Black Folks.'"

The next day Grace, sitting at her window at the hotel, after supper, glancing over the daily papers, was startled by a heinous yell. Looking out, she saw four white men dragging a poor Negro to the park, which faced the hotel. On their trail a thousand whites followed, crying at the top of their voices:

"Lynch him! Lynch him!"

She had heard and read much of lynchings, but never thought she would witness such a barbarous scene, enacted by her own people. Yet, here was a poor fellow,—perhaps innocent of the crime with which he was charged,—being brutally killed, without being able to utter one single word in defense of himself.

Quickly they strung him up to a tree and, daubing his body with pitch, struck fire to him. In telling of the fiendish deed afterward, Grace said:

"The sight was too brutal for words. Soon the sizzling and crackling of the fire could be heard, and the smell of human flesh was stifling. I wanted to satisfy myself that real people were implicated in the deed, but as I looked upon the upturned faces it seemed as if the spirit of humanity had fled from that mob and that in its stead a living devil was implanted. 'Oh!' thought I, 'I cannot dwell another night among these people.' So, in my excitement, I packed my grip and went to the office to settle my bill. After having done so, and while waiting for transportation to the depot, I encountered the same man whom I had met on the previous day. He quickly recognized me and said with a laugh:

" 'I am sure glad you are going, miss; for we will certainly have to string up another Nigger to-morrow.' Then he gave a fiendish chuckle and passed on."

Grace never bore any hatred in her heart for any one, but this man, Joe Vardam, had created within her a most uncomfortable feeling.

A few moments after her encounter with him she was whirled off to the depot. Reaching there, she found that she had leisure on her hands before her train was due. She wondered just how to pass away the time. She wanted to talk with a real sympathizer, or with one, who, even if he were not a sympathizer, possessed a tinge of respect for his community and had ideals. Looking around the partly filled depot, she saw no promise in the faces of those around her. Her eye was attracted toward the door, and there she saw an immaculately

THE LYNCHING 41

dressed man of middle age,—tall and symmetrical of frame,—with the air of a born aristocrat. He was ushered in by a black lad who seemed to be showing him every attention. After he had arranged for his baggage, the lad left him, courteously bowing.

"Surely," thought Grace, "this is a man I can talk to,—one from whom I may gain information regarding these parts that no one whom I have yet seen would willingly give me."

Before he had espied her, she arose, and as the bench upon which he sat had only one other occupant, she quickly sat there, waiting for an opportunity to speak.

The aristocrat, as soon as his eyes rested upon Grace, regarded her with deep interest.

"Pardon me," he said; "are you an Ennery?"

"Yes," she quietly replied, fearful lest he might discern her eagerness to talk.

"You came here, I suppose, to visit your ——" he paused.

"Uncle," Grace quickly replied.

"Oh, yes," said he; "then Francis was your father? We were boys together, and our parents were good friends."

Grace found herself drawing very near to the opportunity for which she longed,—to be able to glean the information she desired.

"How do you like the South?" asked her companion.

"Not at all," she answered. "I am going home sooner than I anticipated, because of the crime perpetrated before my eyes."

"Oh, the lynching, you mean. That has become a common occurrence in these parts, I regret to say."

"I regret to say," meant worlds to Grace. It made her feel that she had met a sympathizer.

CHAPTER VI

SANTA MARIA, PAST AND PRESENT

"I AM so glad to hear you talk thus," remarked Grace. "If it would not seem inquisitive, I wish you would tell me why the Blacks have so little protection in a country so unique in its Republican form of government. I have always loved my country, and even though I knew conditions were not so very good in the South, I did not understand it to be a condition that resulted from gross injustice on the part of my people towards a people powerless to protect themselves."

"My dear Miss Ennery, you are too conscientious in this matter, I fear. We all would like to see the millennium if we could but the world is not ready for it yet."

"We may not be ready for the millennium," interrupted Grace, "but we should at all times use our consciences. Right is right, sir. Oh, pardon me if I have been too bold. Of course you know that I am a Northerner, and while, for so young a woman, I may express myself in too frank terms regarding my attitude toward your treatment of the Blacks here, yet I feel that I am justified because they are human beings and our brothers; and we are our brothers' keepers."

Mr. Garrett assured Grace that she was justified in all she had said, and that her view was no different from that of the average Northerner. Yet even the Northerner, he went on, after residing in the South for a time, often became more bitter in his attitude toward the Blacks than were those that had always lived there.

Along came the train, and emerging from some inconspicuous corner, the black boy, who assisted Mr. Garrett some time before, came forward to be of further service to his employer. Mr. Garrett, speaking very kindly, bade him take Grace's luggage to the car and arrange her comfortably.

At parting with her recent acquaintance, Grace said:

"I thank you so much, sir, for your patience in answering my questions. I shall go away with a different impression than I would have had had I not met you."

"You flatter me, Miss Ennery. I am the one who has been benefited. I would like to, at this moment,—if I had the power,—make such laws as would give every black man, woman, and child better protection. Since we have had this

PAST AND PRESENT 45

pleasant little chat, and also since your father and I are good friends,—also your uncle,—I trust you may give me the privilege of hunting you up on the train, and continuing this conversation, if it is agreeable to you.''

"I shall be delighted," replied Grace.

So, giving her one of his cards, the old aristocrat handed her over to his body-servant, who courteously escorted her to her seat.

The car was well on its way to the North, and Grace had settled herself quite comfortably, when Mr. Garrett found his childhood chum's daughter. Grace was much impressed with her new-found friend, and waited, with profound anticipation, to hear what of interest he had to tell her.

Before delving into the all-important question, he told her that he was on his way to the governor of the State to report on the recent lynching, which was a great source of grief to the committee of which he was a member. This committee, he further stated, consisted of a group of men, selected by the governor, who met after such disturbances as lynchings and riots, passed judgment upon them, and reported their findings to the governor.

"Why can you not stop such riots before they go as far as they did this afternoon?"

"A lynching-bee is often gotten up so suddenly that frequently in one hour it is both planned and executed. When we are able to jail the victim, we are more likely to protect his body."

"Please tell me," Grace asked, "how things ever developed to this state of affairs, in this beautiful settlement, where nature's artist has painted so lavishly, the skies, the bay, and the trees, and where everything is bathed in an atmosphere of serenity."

Settling himself comfortably and clearing his throat so that he might be distinctly heard above the rumbling of the train, Seward Garrett began:

"In 1870 the Negro was given the ballot in this State. About that time a Negro was made secretary of the State. A number of colored men also went to Congress. Negro legislators held regal sway in the capitol, with their mahogany tables, Brussels carpets, and Dresden china cuspidors. At the change of administration, in 1876, the Federal troops that protected the rights of the Negro were withdrawn from this State, and when other complications came up between Republicans and Democrats, the Southern Confederates took possession of the State capitol by force. Then came the Kuklux Klans. They were oath-bound societies, the members disguised with masks and armed to the teeth. They rode at night, committed depredations, and did their bloody work. They

PAST AND PRESENT 47

intimidated Negro voters, drove them by force from the polls, and suppressed the Negro leaders until eventually the constitutions of the Southern States practically disfranchised the race. But in spite of all these drawbacks, the Negro rose intellectually and financially. Of course you have heard of the Leader's school.''

''Yes, I have been on the grounds,'' interposed Grace.

''Well, then, you saw what, in spite of great opposition, he accomplished. He was forced, because of the interference of the Democrats here,—who hold political sway, of course,—to cut out all of the higher courses from the curriculum. This has been a great blow to the Blacks, as nothing above the elementary grades can be taught now.''

''Do you not think this very unfair, Mr. Garrett?''

''Well, I suppose you do; but down here they do not think the Negro ready for the higher stuff yet.''

''Well then, the politicians are supposed to be the judges as to when the brain can accept certain branches of information. If they are able to determine this, then they know more than all the seers ever knew. Mr. Garrett, few human beings have ever desired anything along intellectual lines unless they were ready for it. 'Tis sad to blight the higher bent of man, 'tis cruel,—man must at all times, to develop the highest within him, be a free agent. Oh, 'tis all wrong, all wrong!''

"It may be, but time will tell. And remember, Miss Ennery, the worst enemies of the Blacks are not the descendants of their former owners, but a class of poor whites who have pushed in from the mountains, and who never knew of them, other than that they crowded them out of a livelihood, by having the monopoly of service. This condition, of course, kept them very poor, barely above starvation; hence this is the cause of their intense prejudice. These people prospered after Emancipation, and to-day are the life, politically and commercially, of the South. The Negro, it is true, was caught in a mesh that he is still untangling. It is evident that the only satisfactory solution will be for him to find his own way out."

"But how can he do this, without the protection that his country should offer?"

"I don't know, but he must do it some way, Miss Ennery. We Anglo-Saxons surely must have found an opportunity to wedge our way out of the conditions that we first faced generations ago."

"Yes, I know, Mr. Garrett; but these people have a far greater fight than our Anglo-Saxon ancestors had. Saddest of all are the distinct physical characteristics, so unlike ours, that

PAST AND PRESENT 49

make the problem a matter of condition plus color.''

Mr. Garrett, looking at his watch, found that he had nearly reached his destination. So getting up, he wished Miss Ennery a safe journey home, and asked her to come at some future time and visit his home in Santa Maria, where his wife and daughters would be most happy to welcome her.

After Grace had thanked her companion for his courtesy, and, too, for his extreme kindness in explaining matters so plainly as to racial conditions, they parted as the train rolled in to the capital of the State.

CHAPTER VII

GRACE ENNERY'S RETURN TO NEW YORK

Darkness had not yet completely taken possession of the landscape, and Grace sat admiring the Southern sunset,—with its wonderful golden hues,—as it fell upon the autumn foliage, making a most gorgeous display. The skies, so wondrously blue, made Grace wish for her palette and brushes.

"Nature is so generous," she thought; "depriving none of us,—no matter how humble,—of her grandeur!"

Looking away toward the west, she discerned mountains. "Those must be the mountains that Mr. Garrett referred to. There was the home of the 'poor whites,'—made poor by slavery. Surely there must be a law of retribution. In crushing the slave our own people were crushed, because an inferior element sprang up,—an element that would never have come into existence but for the importation of slaves."

After traveling a day and a night, Grace reached New York. Mr. and Mrs. Grant met her at the station. They were whirled quickly

GRACE ENNERY'S RETURN 51

home; and she, being quite fatigued, without saying very much of her trip, went directly to bed.

Before going to sleep she wondered what she could do to help the colored people; for she determined to do something for them. Never having made a study of the sentiment of the North with regard to this race, and not knowing to what extent prejudice existed, she resolved to find out. In a way she had been removed, nearly all her life, from the world at large, because of her mother's death. In a select boarding-school one would hardly hear of the Negro and his condition, and similar problems, discussed to any extent.

Grace thought that she would try to find out the Grant family's opinion regarding the question that dominated her young mind.

This family consisted, beside Mr. and Mrs. Grant, of a girl of twelve, a boy of ten, and a baby girl of four.

"Aunt Grace," said Margaret, the oldest daughter, after dinner the next night, "we missed you so much. We thought that the Niggers had stolen you; didn't we, Mother?"

"No, Margaret, they did not bother me in the least,—in fact, I enjoyed seeing them and talking with them."

"O Aunt Grace, what could you find interesting in these people?"

"A great deal, Margaret. I found them very much like ourselves in every way except color. And in the South, many who were pointed out to me as colored were really as white as you or I."

"They are wicked and bad and were made by the devil," chimed in Jack, who had left off his reading to listen.

While Mrs. Grant,—one of those mothers who experience difficulty in controling her children,—was trying to quiet Margaret and Jack (for she had quickly seen that their attitude was distasteful to Grace), Baby Elleen was singing:

> "Eeny, meeny, miney, mo!
> Catch a Nigger by the toe;
> If he hollers, let 'im go,
> Eeny, meeny, miney, mo!"

"No, children, you must not deride these poor people: their lot is so hard, and they need a helping hand," remarked Grace earnestly.

"O Aunt Grace," remarked Margaret, "I couldn't love a Nigger,—I couldn't."

"Then give them your sympathy," said Grace, rising.

Mr. Grant was not at home, so Grace did not have a chance to sound his views. However, the opportunity was offered the next evening at dinner.

As they sat chatting on various subjects, the

GRACE ENNERY'S RETURN 53

maid announced the fact that the same Nigger who called the other evening was at the door.

"Tell him I don't care to see him, and I don't want him to be ringing my front-door bell again or I'll have him arrested. Wanting me to offer a bill to introduce Niggers into the State militia! Absurd! Niggers with firearms! I'd sooner trust these emigrants that are pouring in upon our shores."

The maid left the room while Mr. Grant was expostulating, and soon Grace heard the front door close with a bang.

Mr. Grant had entered the political arena, while the Great War was on, to protect certain of his Wall Street interests. The war in Europe being over, this country was facing some complicated issues.

Emigration seemed to have reached a serious stage. After the European war, this country, in its generosity, opened its gates without any reservation. To this land came various classes of foreigners to avoid the responsibility that would devolve upon them of building new homes in Europe. Upon this country's investigating a number of plots to blow up various buildings, it was found that anarchists had come over in large numbers. So, in order to avoid the danger that might arise by permitting more of these anarchistic spirits to infest the country, a ban was placed upon emigration. This, of course, was not kindly accepted by many, yet it ultimately became a law.

Then the Negro wanted to serve his country, by admittance into the State militia, where he might be trained as a soldier. This did not meet the approval of many, who were opposed to Negroes' being armed.

These were the pressing questions of the time, and were being seriously discussed.

Mr. Grant, as Grace Ennery saw, was an enemy to her cause. And as such things dawn upon us when we wish to make use of them, she remembered that her father had told her some time ago that he was stopping with folks whom he knew years ago in the South. Now she could see why he spoke thus. She did not comment at all upon his last expression, but discerned in his countenance something that recalled Joe Vardam vividly to her mind.

"I wonder," she thought, but she would wonder no more. She wished to dismiss the dreadful thought from her mind, and said to herself: "No, it cannot be."

After chatting awhile with Mrs. Grant she retired for the night.

While arranging her hair for bed Grace resolved that she would use a portion of her income in behalf of the Blacks. Just how she would do so, she determined to leave to her maturer judgment.

GRACE ENNERY'S RETURN

Grace now became very busy, taking up her work in art, where she had left off. Because Mrs. Grant insisted, she went out occasionally to social functions. Her hostess was a social butterfly, flitting here and there, wherever pleasure could be found. She was happiest when being entertained and entertaining. This, —entertaining,—she was very capable of doing, because her husband provided liberally for her. She had no special aim either for herself or her children. She was continually on the go, and could never understand why Grace would not appreciate her opportunity to mingle in the highest society.

"Grace," she would often say, "you are wasting your youth by not seeing more of life."

"Do you think so, Mrs. Grant?" Grace would reply. "I feel as though I would like to accomplish something before I took up social duties, for I know from observation that I could never do much more than keep up with society, were I to enter it."

"That may be true to some extent; but at your age you should never talk so. With your money and opportunity, many a girl would consider herself blessed."

Then the maid would announce Mrs. De Allen or Count Van Silver, or Fanny de Forest, and away Mrs. Grant would glide bedecked in silks and diamonds, worn with dignity supreme upon a super-stately figure, crowned with a madonna-like face. Whereupon Grace would betake herself to her own apartment, unless requested by Mrs. Grant to stay and meet her distinguished guests. Then she would be agreeable, because she felt that she must.

CHAPTER VIII

THE LETTER THAT FAILED

In her art work Grace Ennery was by no means mediocre. She attracted attention on her return from abroad by a beautiful painting of two children entitled "Love." In the picture one of the children, a boy, climbs an appletree to bring down the last apple,—far out on a frail branch,—to the girl.

Frederick Trower, a patron of art, contributing generously to the cultivation of the fine arts in New York City, was attracted toward Grace, and during her previous stay in the city had called upon her frequently.

During the war Mr. Trower was called abroad to protect the interests of his father in Paris, and from time to time Grace would receive some word from him,—as she would from her father, who was at this time in Egypt. Not very long after her arrival home from the South, Grace found at her place at breakfast a letter postmarked "Paris." She hastily ate and returned to her room to read it. The portion that had the greatest weight with her read as follows:

I don't know what your attitude is toward the Negro, but you may be interested in knowing that the French army has enlisted many of these black men in the ranks, and the report is that they make brave soldiers, going into the hottest of the fray, without reserve or fear.

One herculean black was given a medal of honor a couple of weeks ago, for his bravery in battle. His physique was magnificent,—tall, erect of stature, and well proportioned. He impressed one as he stood to receive his degree. The French people could not do enough for him. Imagine my attending a banquet in his honor! The French seemed to have forgotten his color, and spoke only of his valor and bravery.

After all, Grace, I feel that we Americans are too narrow in our feelings. What difference does it make whether bravery is garbed in black or white? It is deeper than the skin. It reaches the soul, and the soul of the good is always white.

I know you have come in touch with these black people of the South. Tell me your opinion as gained by your trip.

Grace, after reading this interesting letter from Fred Trower, unconsciously wiped her eyes, and held the missive to her lips.

"I have decided," she said half aloud. "I have decided to act upon my convictions. The light that I have desired has been given to me."

Immediately she sat down and wrote a letter to Tom Brinley's mother, in care of the Institute, as she had failed to get Tom's address in her excitement in leaving.

Now, in Santa Maria politics had control of everything. Even the mails of colored people were continually being tampered with.

It happened that the day Grace's letter reached Santa Maria, Joe Vardam was lounging around the post office as he usually did. As his money was made more or less from political

THE LETTER THAT FAILED 59

graft, he often, when he had time on his hands, helped Billy, the postmaster, sort the mail. In coming across this letter marked "New York," and written in a legible hand to Tom Brinley's mother, Joe Vardam became curious.

He had always had a suspicious feeling regarding this fellow. He watched the development of his precocious mind with envy, as he feared he might attract attention, especially among those who were Negro sympathizers. Often he shook his fist at the boy and told him to keep scarce.

As soon as Joe Vardam discovered the letter he told Billy that he would deliver it. Briskly walking to his cottage, where he lived alone, and stealthily entering it, as if he feared even his own conscience, he lit a kerosene lamp and hastily read the following words:

MY DEAR MRS. BRINLEY:
I have been thinking of Tom ever since my return. I wanted so much to talk with you about him, but the dreadful lynching hastened my departure.
I want to educate Tom, and send him abroad if necessary. I want to help him develop the splendid nascent manhood which slumbers in his nature.

After reading this much, Joe Vardam chuckled.

"Ah, my dear woman, you will be baffled this time. You'll not get your wish, if I can balk it."

Joe Vardam was a politician of the lowest

type. There was nothing too degrading for him to do in order to gain his ends.

It was whispered that he had beaten his poor wife to death, and that he drove his son from home, when the latter would not coöperate with him in political wrongs. Where the younger Vardam went no one knew.

It was also whispered that Joe Vardam's father, a very cruel slaveholder, was killed by one of his slaves, because he thrashed a woman slave until she became unconscious. The slave in turn thrashed him, and when Vardam's father drew his pistol to shoot him, the slave wrested it from his hand and shot the master. Then the homicide gave himself up to the authorities to be dealt with as they saw fit.

Joe Vardam, whether because of the manner of his father's death was seeking vengeance or because of the natural cruelty that possessed him, was relentless wherever a Negro was concerned. For some reason he held a bitter hatred for the race.

After thinking over the letter during the night, Joe Vardam determined to place Tom Brinley where he would never attract attention. Day after day he walked the streets of Santa Maria in search of his prey, wishing to catch him away from his home and surroundings. Not many days had passed by when he found his opportunity. Noticing that the

THE LETTER THAT FAILED 61

Leader's grave was bare, and not having enough money to buy suitable flowers, Tom, after school one day, told his mother that he was going over to San Joan to gather wild flowers for the Leader's grave. Just as he was about to embark across the stream in a little rowboat, which he found on the sands of Santa Maria, he was seized by the collar by Vardam and dragged back to the settlement.

"All right, you little rascal, you will hang around stealin' boats and idlin' your time away,—will you? I'll fix you. To the chain-gang with you!"

When Tom Brinley's mother heard of her child's arrest, she tried in every way to reach the proper authorities, in order to speak a word in behalf of her son. The way seemed barred, for she was told that what Joe Vardam had passed judgment upon could not be changed. In her great grief she decided to leave Santa Maria and seek the North, as she had now lost all hope. She had saved a little money for Tom's schooling. This she took. After closing up her home in which she had spent so many happy days both with her husband and her boy,—she took the boat for New York, where she hoped to get something to do to try to forget her great affliction. Her friends sympathized with her and kept her in touch with all that was transpiring in Santa Maria.

Her kindly, sympathetic face won for her a good home with the de Forest family, who had advertised for a good laundress.

One day Miss de Forest had a young people's party, and among the invited guests were the little Grants. Running around, as children will, Elleen roamed into the kitchen, where she came across Mandy Brinley, who was sobbing. Soon the child had assembled all the other little ones at the door to watch the sobbing woman.

At the Grants' supper-table that night the children told of the colored woman's crying in Miss de Forest's kitchen; at which Grace expressed great sympathy.

"Aunt Grace," said Margaret Grant, "her son was stolen in the South by a cruel man and put on the chain-gang."

"That is very sad," answered Grace. "Suppose Jack were to be taken from us suddenly, without warning, and we were never to see him again?"

"Oh, that would be awful!" chimed little Elleen. "Is some one going to steal our Jack?"

"I'll shoot them," said the little fellow, by way of defending himself.

CHAPTER IX

THE PROPOSAL

Days and weeks passed and still Grace received no reply to the letter she had sent. She could not determine what she was to do next. In the meantime she still worked at her art, expending her greatest efforts in the painting of a likeness of Tom Brinley (as nearly as was possible), a painting that she named "Purpose."

A member of the F. N. P. (Federation For Negro Protection,—a group of influential Whites and Blacks, formed for the protection of the rights of the black man in the North and the South), seeing the picture, asked that it be loaned for an exhibition that they were about to give. Grace gladly consented to this, and the picture was placed in the Gallery of Fine Arts.

Nanna, the old cook at the de Forests' house, by way of making it pleasant for Mandy Brinley, asked her to attend the exhibit with her. This Nanna was a woman who stood for the highest aims of the Blacks,—with which race she was identified. Often she would say,

"I'm a cook, an' I'm not ashamed of my daily occupation, for a good cook must take pride in her work; yet I would not see all my people laboring in this field. They must scatter themselves in all avenues of work, in order to become a well-rounded, well-developed people. I am always anxious to know what all my people are doing."

Hence her interest in the exhibit, which marked an anniversary of progress for her people.

The great armory where the exhibition was held was crowded,—the F. N. P. having also invited a number of speakers, both white and black, to talk in behalf of the Negro. The absorbing themes were, "The Negro In Office," "The Negro In Politics," and "The Negro In The Army."

How Mandy Brinley wished for her Tom; and in walking about after the great addresses, she, as if her prayer was answered, came face to face with a painted reproduction of her Tom.

"O my Jesus!" she cried, "Nanna, here's my boy,—here's my Tom!"

"Go on, Mandy; you've got your boy on your mind so you imagine everything is him."

Grace Ennery and Fred Trower were also present. They almost passed Tom Brinley's mother as she turned from the picture in great grief. Grace in her absorption in other exhib-

THE PROPOSAL

its did not see Mandy. But Fred Trower saw her, and he remarked to himself that the wonderful eyes of the lad must have made her sad.

Nanna and Mandy returned quietly home,—Mandy laden with sorrow. Grace and Fred, after the interesting meeting, sauntered leisurely home. They talked of the speakers, especially the Negro speakers, who knew what their people needed.

"I am sure Tom Brinley would do equally as well as any of those speakers, were he given the opportunity to develop himself," said Grace. "It is so strange that I never received any reply to my first letter to his mother,—and my second was returned to me."

Fred replied:

"Grace, I am afraid you are taking matters too seriously. Sometimes those whom we would wish to be worthy are altogether unworthy."

"Not so with Tom; he has a strong will, and I am quite sure that he, although young, has determined to develop in the direction of his natural taste and aptitude."

"Now, Grace, I begin to think that you never intend to devote any of your time to me. Since I have returned home, you have had this and that to interfere with our pleasant little chats,—such as we use to have."

"Forgive me, Fred, if I have appeared selfish since you have returned. It is not selfishness; it is really that my life is broader. Unexpected problems have come before me, and I am anxious to grapple with them."

Whether Grace knew it or not, Fred Trower was in love with her, and had been so even before she went abroad to study art. Whenever the desire urged him to say something of his tenderness to her, her mind seemed always centered on something else, which made any declaration of love at that time quite inopportune.

When they had reached home, Fred asked Grace to give him an evening and to promise him for once not to speak of any of her pet hobbies, but to give up the entire time to him.

"It is a small favor, Fred," answered Grace. "You may have your wish, of course."

"All right, I shall see you to-morrow evening. And if Mrs. Grant has company, be prepared for a walk, as these evenings are very enticing in the open."

"Very well. Good-night," said Grace, as she endeavored to disengage her arm.

Instead of freeing the arm immediately, however, Fred Trower pressed it gently and looked into her large blue eyes, which, with upturned gaze, met his. The look was like the meeting of two souls,—each read the heart of the other. Quickly Grace, as if she had committed a mis-

THE PROPOSAL

deed, went into the vestibule, remaining there until the maid admitted her. The maid noticed a flushed look upon Grace's face, as she thanked the girl and ran swiftly to her own apartment.

Fred Trower stood for a moment as if glued to the spot. Then, collecting himself, he turned and hastened away.

Grace, when she reached her luxuriously appointed apartment,—consisting of bed-room, private sitting-room, and bath,—yielded to an irresistible impulse to run to the bay-window of her sitting-room, which permitted her to see a distance up the street. There she sat, hat and coat on, watching pass on under the bright electric lights the manly, erect form of the man about whom was now the glamour of a young girl's love. When he had passed out of sight she slowly disrobed, and went to bed,— thinking of many things that before this night had never seriously entered her mind. To-night Tom Brinley had no place in her young mind. Hers was a dream of love, with Fred Trower crowned king.

The next day seemed to two persons the longest day upon the calendar; and when the sun was slowly sinking in the west, two hearts were beating with gladness.

Grace was ready long before the maid announced Mr. Trower. Fred was prepared long before he came. His father noticed the new light in Fred's eye, as he closed the lid of his desk and hurried off, calling back:

"Good-night, Dad."

His father's look followed him to the door, and he questioned:

"Something on to-night, Fred?"

But his son was gone.

When the maid did announce the presence of Fred Trower in the parlors below, the fact had already been known to Grace some time. She was seated behind her curtain, on her window-seat, waiting,—in accordance with the demands of society,—to be told what she already knew.

Softly she stole downstairs,—so much more softly than was her custom,—and, with an air of coquettishness, sat opposite her lover. No word had yet been broken, when Fred, full of ardor, and not knowing how to free his pent-up feeling, rose and bent over her, saying:

"Grace, you know it all, do you not? Need I tell you how tenderly I love you? You do care for me some, do you not?"

Grace held her head back, and looking into Fred's eyes, replied softly:

"Yes, Fred; I think I do."

Then his head bent lower, and their lips met, after which Fred sat beside Grace, her hand in his and their heads together. Fred told her of his great love for her, how he hoped that it

THE PROPOSAL

would be reciprocated; he also told her of his splendid prospects, and asked if she would consent to become his wife.

Grace answered:

"Not yet, Fred. I must do something of worth before I accept the very tender care that I know you are capable of giving me. Let me devote more time to my art before anything definite is decided."

"Why, Grace, you have done something! What more commendation can you wish than has been given to your pictures,—"Love" and "Purpose"?

"But that is just a beginning, Fred. Then there is Tom Brinley. Must I leave him? Should I not try to find him and help him?"

"Then, may I hope that you may tell me something definite as to our final plans when this little colored boy is found? As to your art, Grace, you can do even better work after you marry. A woman is better able to express herself, whatever her sphere in life, after she marries, because her life includes a broader scope. About the lad: my father wants me to look into some cotton interests in the South soon, and I can extend my trip, visit the Institute, and inquire about the boy."

"Dear Fred, you are so considerate, and I am so thankful that you will do this. I have a peculiar feeling concerning this boy, some inner prompting that urges me on."

"Well, don't worry any more, Grace. Everything will come out satisfactorily. So you have really decided to educate this colored lad?"

"Yes, Fred; my desire is to give him an opportunity to serve his people."

"I trust that he will prove himself worthy of your interest."

"I am sure he will. By the way, Fred, I received a letter from my father, who is in Egypt now. He spoke very highly of you, and much of his friendship with your father. He says that his stay will be an extended one, as the Egyptian climate agrees with him better than any other that he has been in. He speaks in glowing terms of the scenery of the Nile, and has been captivated by the grandeur of Egypt's monuments. He has seen the pyramids, the Memnonion Colossi, the Temple of the kings at Luxor, and the vast Hypostile Hall at Karnak. He also writes that my uncle has joined him, having attended to his business affairs in Europe. How glad I shall be when he returns!"

"When I write and tell him of our plans, I shall insist upon his returning for our wedding, which I trust will be in the near future."

They finished the evening with happy talk

THE PROPOSAL 71

on topics that would naturally be of interest to engaged couples.

Fred Trower was overjoyed. The fact that Grace Ennery had truly agreed to share her future with him made him show his delight without any reserve. He was a handsome fellow of about twenty-eight,—nearly seven years Grace's senior,—yet there was something quite boyish in his air to-night, Grace thought as she looked at him admiringly: his complexion was so clear, his soft brown eyes so full of sympathy. Eyes and hair were so exactly of the same shade that one wondered how nature could match in humanity her colors so harmoniously.

Any one gazing at the man at Grace Ennery's side,—with his hair slightly ruffled, looking admiringly into the girl's face,—would at once recognize and be amused at the boyishness portrayed in his manner, and would consider him not so bad for an only child, humored and petted as only children usually are.

Time flew by so rapidly that it quite surprised the young lovers when they heard the hall clock strike eleven.

When Frederick Trower rose to go, he looked so pleadingly at Grace that she could not resist going over to him and throwing her golden head upon his breast and permitting him to caress it with all the fondness that his manly nature could display. Then he left her with her promise, that a date of marriage would be set as soon as Tom Brinley's future had been arranged for.

A few weeks later Fred Trower left for the South.

CHAPTER X

FRED TROWER IN THE SOUTH

After reaching Richmond and arranging business matters, in accordance with his father's suggestions, Fred took the train for further South.

The South was not new to him. He had been there a number of times, as his father had various financial interests in different sections of the country; yet he had never been there bent on the mission he had now undertaken,—the search of a poor little brown lad.

All along the road he studied the people, —especially at the depots, which seemed a veritable "hang-out."

"I wonder," thought he, "if these people will ever carve out their own destiny? Judging from these laggards, who seem utterly dependent, one would say not."

These were merely passing thoughts, and Fred did not allow them to worry him seriously. He felt that Grace had enough philanthropy for them both.

After an extremely hot and dusty trip, he reached Santa Maria. He took a carriage, and having reached the hotel, went directly to his apartments, as he felt very dusty and tired.

In the morning, which was an extremely warm one, he awoke early. After breakfast he walked around town and was attracted by the beauty of the place. Roses were in bloom and nature had everywhere a glad, smiling look.

Quite an inquisitive gaze was bestowed upon Fred when he asked at the hotel:

"What is the best time to visit the Vance Institute?"

The clerk quickly replied:

"We don't know much about them Niggers; they stay over on that side, and we stay on this. Nobody much bothers about them. They tell me that the school is going to the dogs. You came down to look 'em over, I suppose."

"Yes," said Fred, not wishing to prolong the conversation with this somewhat contrary individual.

He passed out of the hotel door and went down the steps, walking off somewhat slowly down the street. He had not gone very far when a somewhat repulsive looking man, tall, middle-aged, and carelessly attired, overtook him.

"Lookin' us folks behind the sun over, I suppose?" he ventured.

"Well, somewhat," replied Fred. "You have a pretty nice town here."

FRED TROWER IN THE SOUTH 75

"Yes, but things have gone somewhat to the dogs, on account of these lazy darkies down this way. Can't make 'em work unless you beat 'em. There's that fine school that fool Vance put up for 'em, an' they don't even have enough attendin' to keep the doors open."

"Are you acquainted around these parts?" asked Fred,—for he thought that he might get the information he desired from this man.

"Yes I know everybody in and aroun' Santa Maria,—white an' black."

"Then you probably know something of a Tom Brinley?"

"That little black thief an' idler? Of course I do. What do you want with him?"

"I am trying to find him for a friend of mine."

"Well, you won't come across him 'round these parts. He was sent to the chain-gang in the backwoods for idlin' and stealin'."

Fred did not seem as shocked as one might think at hearing this, for all along the road, he had seen the Negro's idleness. And since theft follows such a weakness, it seemed just natural.

"What did your friend wish with this little black devil?" asked Vardam, for it was he.

"She thought that she saw some good traits in him and wished to develop them."

"What Nigger has any but bad traits? A

woman too! Good Lord! My good man, keep her away from Niggers, or she and you will regret it some day."

Fred never found the Institute, in fact he had no desire to hunt for it, after talking with this man. He lit a cigar, and puffing it complacently, slowly returned to his hotel.

On the veranda he stopped to watch the Southern sunset. Slowly and slowly Old Sol sank to the western horizon, and when almost all had disappeared, the rest dropped suddenly out of sight. As Fred Trower witnessed this sudden dropping, he thought of how Grace's fond hopes had vanished like a dream.

He said to himself:

"It's all tomfoolery her coming down here and getting interested in a trifling black lad, who was not worth a rap. Anyhow, I have done my part. I wish Grace would not get so wrapped up in these good-for-nothing people."

After staying around another day, Fred started for home. He ran into a college chum, who was traveling in the interest of an agricultural society, and he persuaded Fred to attend this Farmers' Conference with him.

Jerry Dill did not mention the fact that this conference concerned the Blacks as well as the Whites; for if he did, I do not think Fred Trower would have troubled to go.

FRED TROWER IN THE SOUTH

He was not a narrow man,—he tried to view a subject from all sides before arriving at a conclusion; yet he failed to see anything other than absurdity in his errand to Santa Maria. When his friend, Jerry Dill, found that Fred had some time to spare, he persuaded him to attend the Farmers' Conference,—not that Fred Trower was one bit interested in farms or farmers nor did he have any special desire to hang around the South; but the air was somewhat balmy and his love for nature met its response in everything in bloom. So Fred told Jerry that if it were not for the tugging at his heartstrings that drew him home, he would like to remain in the sunny South for an indefinite time.

The friends alighted at a little town, about seventy miles from Richmond, called Hollis, and found a pleasant little boarding-place. After Jerry had made all necessary arrangements for the following day he and Fred roamed around the village for a little fresh air.

As they wandered off the main road, they came to a settlement of cabins, behind which were richly cultivated tracts of land. At the doors of the cabins groups of blacks were congregated.

"This settlement," said Jerry, "is one of the most progressive in the South. The Negroes are very energetic, and this section produces larger crops for its size than any other known settlement.''

"How do you account for this unusual progress here?" asked Fred.

"Well, I suppose the main thing is that these people get better treatment,—that is, there are fairer laws and a better spirit on the part of the authorities here than elsewhere. It's only a matter of human treatment after all, Fred,— the better you treat a horse, the more he will love you and the more devotedly he will serve you."

Even with what Jerry had said, Fred was still reticent in talking of his prime mission in the South. He did not state his own opinions but simply allowed Jerry to air his ideas, and now and then he would inject a question or two of his own.

"Who attends these conferences, and what good is derived from them?" asked Fred.

Jerry replied:

"Well, as I said, a mutual feeling exists between the races down here on matters of mutual concern. All attend the conferences and one gleans information from the other's experiences. That is why this agricultural society sent me down here. They selected this place because they feel that where race hatred is least bitter more good will be developed. As you know, hatred, be it of races or individuals, re-

FRED TROWER IN THE SOUTH

tards progress. This is why I feel that the South is behind the North,—because it spends a good bit of its time and valuable energy trying to crush the blacks politically and otherwise."

Fred still did not comment but listened attentively. Soon the two retraced their steps, and until a late hour sat upon the boarding-house veranda and smoked: Jerry dreaming of the excellent reports he would be able to take back to the Agricultural Society, and Fred dreaming of Grace, the girl of his heart, and of her disappointment when she should hear the bad news of her would-be protégé, Tom Brinley.

After the two, amid circles of smoke, had dreamed to their heart's content, they went contentedly to bed.

CHAPTER XI

THE FARMERS' CONFERENCE

The next morning when Fred Trower awoke he wondered what impressions he would gain before the day was over. His disappointment had been so great that he had not written to Grace since his arrival in Santa Maria. Rising late, he missed Jerry, who had left a note stating that he would be found at Town Hall, where the conference would be held. Fred ate his breakfast leisurely, then wrote a note to Grace, stating that he would tell her everything as soon as he should reach home, which would be in a few days, and that at this writing he was attending, with a college chum, a farmers' conference at the place mentioned. After mailing his letter, he walked leisurely toward the Town Hall.

As Fred approached the Hall he saw the most interesting sight he ever witnessed in his life. Every kind of vehicle that could be mentioned stood outside the place and, upon looking in different directions, he still saw more coming. Some,—the better situated financially,—came

THE FARMERS' CONFERENCE 81

in autos and others came on horseback. Occasionally, the father, mother, and child were carried on one poor horse. Then others came in wagons, in shays, on mules, and in ox-carts.

The colored women were dressed in every bright color one could think of. Some wore hats, with style and without style. Red bandannas seemed to have the day among them. The styles effected by the men were various. Vests were in as many colors as were the women's dresses. And Prince Alberts were almost in as great evidence among the men as red bandannas were among the women. Fred did not know whether he was attending a farmers' conference or a Baptist convention.

When he entered the hall, he saw a goodly number, both white and colored, seated. Many seemed to be conferring, one with the other, and, to his surprise, the atmosphere was most genial. Jerry Dill had seen his friend enter and take his place amid the crowd of farmers, and knowing that Fred would enjoy the sight better from the platform, he sent down for him.

"Some style!" said Fred to Jerry as he was escorted to a seat.

"Yes, old pal; but just you wait and see what they know. Just listen and hear what Dame Nature has taught them. What they know from that sincere teacher would surprise some of our fair lads and lassies in high school."

The meeting was called to order by the moderator. As Fred looked around him, he was surprised to see the class of men that had come to listen to the farming experiences of these illiterate country folk.

The meeting lagged somewhat at first, as one would naturally expect. The innocent country folk had to be aroused, just as the little seeds and plants need to be drawn out of the earth by the sun.

At length one large colored woman arose and told how she was supporting her five children by growing cotton.

" 'Tis de swelles' cotton dat grows anywheres aroun'!" she cried enthusiastically.

She told of how the land had been at first a hollow pond, of how her boys had filled it in and fertilized it, and of her great success.

Black speakers and white were interspersed, but Fred found the Negroes far more interesting, because of their ingenious ways of doing things.

He listened with enthusiasm to a colored farmer whose clothes were less gaudy than any of the rest. The moderator introduced him as the richest Negro for one hundred miles around.

The speaker arose, and in an unassuming manner spoke of his rise from poverty. He told of his father's and mother's being slaves, and of his being taken away from them when

THE FARMERS' CONFERENCE 83

he was quite young, and of their being sold and going away, and of his never seeing them again. He told of how he would watch the soil and study the growth of things, and of his great success in raising cotton, and how to-day he shipped more cotton of the finer grade than any other farmer in the South.

Fred whispered to Jerry:

"It's wonderful, Jerry, I must admit."

Another burly black man told of the planting of the legumes and of the plowing of the roots under the soil, enriching it with nitrogen, which produced the element necessary for the growth of a number of plants and vegetables that he called by name. He also spoke of the rotation of the crops, thus preventing taking from the soil the same mineral matter year after year. He said that planting different crops every year kept the soil rich for the next crop.

After a few more talks all present filed out to the grounds for dinner.

"A picnic in the biggest sense!" thought Fred.

Jerry took Fred around among the farmers, showing him the cooked materials, all of which had been raised by them.

Fred remarked afterward to his Northern friends,

"Everything looked too good to be true. As

for fried chicken,—many of the colored farmers' wives had it over the French chefs of the Waldorf-Astoria.''

The next morning Fred thanked his friend Jerry and left Hollis for the North, feeling that his trip South had not been such a failure after all.

CHAPTER XII

TOM BRINLEY IN CHAINS

Tom Brinley, grieved to his soul, lay upon a hay bed, in a broken-down little hut,—a figure to move any one to pity. Chained to him was an old man,—Uncle Abbott,—seventy years of age, whom the cruel overseer always used to break in young prisoners. Uncle Abbott took mightily to the boy and urged him not to show much strength, as it would go hard with him. Thus, Tom reserved his energy as directed by his adviser, and well it was that he did, for he was to stand in great need of it later on.

Vardam and Tilton were in league with other political leaders to keep down those Negroes who manifested any degree of independence. These, they branded as "dangerous characters." It was their usual plan to trump up some charge of misdemeanor and then send them to the chain-gang in order to keep the others in the community in submission.

Tilton incarcerated Uncle Abbott because he pastored a set of his people who were always in fear of their employers. Uncle Abbott taught them never to stand in fear of any one but God. These people were so ignorant that they continued to serve their old master in the same capacity as they had in slavery, not really knowing that they had ever been freed. This knowledge was kept from them by their white employers, and it was agreed among these employers to keep them ever thus. Tilton was a political demagogue in these quarters, and pronounced judgment against any one that tried to enlighten the people otherwise.

Thus, Uncle Abbott posed as merely the preacher for these people; but secretly he had a knowledge of their ignorance, and, with an assumption of shrewdness, effected to teach them humility. When not spied upon, however, he told them of their freedom,—of Lincoln and the Emancipation, teaching them, too, their rights. The effect was soon seen. A number of the Blacks left Holding for other climes.

When Tilton heard of this, he questioned Uncle Abbott, who replied:

"Yes, I told my people of their freedom; and now my work is done. You may do whatever you wish with me. It was my mission, and now it has been fulfilled."

"To the chain-gang with you!" cried Tilton. "Lynching is too good. I must put you where you can be tortured and tormented,—you deceiving beast!"

TOM BRINLEY IN CHAINS 87

Thus Uncle Abbott was sent to the chain-gang, and had been there two years when Tom Brinley came. Two favors he asked of his incarcerators,—to be able to take his worn and torn Bible, and a little grip that held a few pieces of worn clothing. His wish was granted.

When Uncle Abbott went to Holding to preach, he had taken with him money, which was hidden between the worn covers of his Bible, for he did not know when he might be forced to leave. Thus he could depend upon this money which he had saved to get away with, should the opportunity be offered to him. When he found that he did not have the chance to escape, as he had anticipated, he resignedly faced the situation. He had almost forgotten that he had this money, when Tom came upon the scene.

After he had heard Tom's sad story from the boy's own lips, and had discerned his aptitude and indomitable spirit,—which would mean much to his people,—he determined to help the lad make his escape.

Uncle Abbott was not a man of much learning, but he was possessed of tact and a native shrewdness which mastered any emergency. He truly would have made a leader, had he been given the chance. In Tom he saw true worth and appreciated it, and all his mental energy was spent in planning for this boy an escape from a life of torture.

"Here is worth," he would say to himself as he would watch the boy asleep. "It must not let its life-blood be sapped in these backwoods. My people are crying for men, and more men. I have had my day,—I have done my Master's bidding. But, Tom, the power of God is greater than the devil. I shall pray for your freedom, and it will surely come."

In his satchel he had a little tool-kit, which no one knew he had there. No one ever watched him, as he had never attempted to make his escape, or the escape of any one else, before, even though he had brought his tools for this purpose. He had heard of this place, and knew that many an innocent man had perished in these chains. And in his profound grief he did not forget that he might have a chance to be of service,—even in the chain-gang.

CHAPTER XIII

TOM BRINLEY'S ESCAPE TO THE NORTH

Uncle Abbott awoke Tom one night, and told him what he intended doing. Tom pleaded with the old man not to jeopardize his own life by trying to assist him. Uncle Abbott told him not to fear, that he knew the road well and that he felt that Divine guidance would clear the way of any obstacles that might arise. As their hut was located right on the road of escape, he told Tom to follow the road, until he came to Toddsville, where he knew a good Christian family, that would shield him from harm.

"Go to them," he said, "and tell them that I sent you, and they will drive you over to Cherry, where you can board a train for Maryland. After reaching there, buy some decent clothes, and go directly to New York,—where you can pass under another name,—and seek work."

Tom listened attentively to Uncle Abbott; he knew that the guards were situated at the other end of the cabins, for they did not consider it necessary to be very watchful of Uncle Abbott, as he never attempted to escape. And even if Tom did, they knew he could not get very far with Uncle Abbott chained to him. No one ever suspected that the old man had in his possession means by which he could undo his chains if he so desired.

In the moonlight Uncle Abbott released Tom's chains, and put into the lad's pocket all the dry bread he could gather. After he had given him the money from between the covers of the Bible and had wished him God-speed, he bade him to go quickly and quietly. This was too much for Tom. He appreciated his friend's great kindness, but he felt that to take the money, which Uncle Abbott might some day need, would be an imposition. He told the old man that he would rather take his chance at finding something to do, and working his way on to New York, than to take that which he might some day need.

But the old man replied:

"No, I will not consider you out of danger until you have crossed the Mason and Dixon line. Prejudice to-day, my boy, is very rank down here, and if you are caught anywhere in the South, I know that they will place you where there will never be any hope. So take this money, and travel as fast as you can to your destination. You will for quite some time be

TOM BRINLEY'S ESCAPE

only a few hours in advance of your pursuers, who will be on your heels as soon as they have discovered that you have escaped. Take these tools and bury them somewhere along the road. Be off, my boy, be off!"

Tom bade the old man good-by, saying:

"I shall never forget you as long as I shall live, Uncle Abbott, and if I should get safely to the North, without interference, I will work hard to acquire the power to some day destroy this place that keeps in chains such good people as you."

Then Tom went out stealthily into the night, in the direction that Uncle Abbott pointed out. When he had gone some distance from the cabin, he heard steps and to his dismay came face to face with one of the guards. As quick as a flash he saw his fate.

"To hesitate means death," thought he. So before the guard had really recognized him, Tom made a dive, similar to a flying tackle in foot-ball, and threw him. The lad seemed for the moment to be endowed with supernatural strength. Before the guard could rise or get him fully in his grasp, Tom dealt him a blow across the head with the tool he had not yet disposed of, and fled.

After that unexpected encounter, Tom in his excitement was on the alert every moment, but he met no one else. He reached Toddsville, bedraggled and dusty, about nine o'clock the following morning. Seeing some men on their way to the fields, he asked them to direct him to Uncle Abbott's friends. This they did without questioning the poor boy, who presented a veritable picture of distress.

When Tom found the people and had told them his sad story and the story of Uncle Abbott, their grief knew no bounds.

Tom had just finished his tale of woe when the folks were startled by loud voices outside. Their suspicion was immediately aroused, so they hid Tom in a load of hay. Then Aunt Fanny and Uncle Joe went on with their work, planning that as soon as they had got rid of these trailers they would get Tom to Cherry as quickly as possible.

Sure enough the voices belonged to those that were hunting for Tom. They yelled to Aunt Fanny, asking her if she had seen a little Nigger come along that way.

"Yes," returned Aunt Fanny "a long time ago, an' he look so queer, I knowed he wus up tu mischief. He asked me where Rootville was, an' I showed him, an' off he trotted."

Now, Rootville was in the opposite direction to Cherry, and after looking through her cabin the men hurried in the direction Aunt Fanny had indicated. When the trailers were out of

TOM BRINLEY'S ESCAPE

sight, she put Tom on horseback and directed him to Cherry, where her sister lived.

When Tom reached Cherry he was nearly exhausted. His story touched Fanny's sister, and after seeing to it that he ate a good meal, she bade him rest until the last train left there for Maryland. The boy's clothes by this time were in a wretched condition and as she had boys of about Tom's age, she managed to find some presentable clothing for him to travel further in. He left Cherry on the last train, which reached Washington about noon the following day, where he planned to make his final dash to the North.

Everything went on well for Tom until he reached Washington. He was just about to alight when he espied one of his pursuers standing not many yards away. Whether he was still looking for him, or whether he was traveling on his own accord, Tom did not know. He evidently seemed to be watching for some one when Tom spied him. He had presence of mind to hide himself under a seat and when every one had left the train, he made his exit in another direction.

Tom remained in Washington several days, desiring to make this place his destination, but there was some unknown impulse that urged him on to the metropolis.

While in Washington, he saw many things of

interest. To him, it was a wonderful city. The streets, so beautifully planned, and the innumerable public buildings impressed him greatly.

At midnight a few evenings afterwards, Tom Brinley was well on his way to New York. Arriving there, he was directed by a porter to a good stopping place. He dreaded telling his secret, as he had been warned that as he traveled farther North he would not find his own people as loyal to him as the simple Southern folks were in their sympathetic hearts. So he kept his secret in his breast, and assumed the name of Frank Hope. Frank was his benefactor's Christian name, and Hope was his own fancy,—for he hoped for better things in the future, as he pursued his eventful career.

Tom Brinley soon found work, and also time to devote to his studies. He never permitted an opportunity for mental improvement to slip by. To his notice soon came Hooper's Institute, with its advantages for the pursuance of studies in the evenings after working hours. This suited Tom admirably. And he could be found at his desk at the Institute in the evening, while during the day he worked.

He attracted much attention, both at work and at the Institute. Yet in his great desire to learn he did not consider that he, because of his application to duty, was being admired by those that came in touch with him.

TOM BRINLEY'S ESCAPE 95

At this time a young colored woman attracted his attention. Tom was now in his seventeenth year. Unassuming and manly, he impressed this modest young colored girl, who, like himself, was taking advantage of an opportunity that the North offered.

One evening as they passed out together, Mary Abbott,—that was her name,—said:

"I have been so interested in this article about this Tom Brinley, whom they are seeking, that I want you to read it."

Tom took the paper calmly and read this headline:

ONE THOUSAND DOLLARS REWARD FOR THE RETURN OF A BLACK BOY WHO IS AN ESCAPED CONVICT.

And then the text went on to give his description as to color, height, looks, and so on.

Whether Mary was suspicious or not, Tom did not know. She told him that the paper had been sent to her from the South by friends, who sympathized with the boy, because they knew that he was innocent. They had also told her that in that section if any colored person chanced to attract attention by being ambitious, he would be put out of the way by political renegades.

Much to his dismay, Tom found that he was not even safe in New York. What should he do? What resort had he? Upon handing the paper back to Mary, he made no comment upon it other than that the victim must either be dangerous or valuable.

Tom found himself occasionally at the side of this fine-looking young girl. He often saw a resemblance to his benefactor, Uncle Abbott, and when she told him of a dear uncle, who was imprisoned by the same wicked people that hunted the boy, he longed to tell her his secret, and how his present opportunity was due to the big-heartedness of this grand old man.

"Not yet," he thought; "I must first know how much she cares for me before I do this. I wish I could tell her of my feeling for her; but I cannot, without telling my secret; so I must keep this, too, within my breast."

One day, while delivering packages for the Bracy firm, for which he worked, Tom came near running into the arms of Joe Vardam. He had one package marked, "Mrs. Silas Grant, East 71st Street." After the maid had taken the package and he was turning to go, he saw Joe Vardam enter the house. The politician did not recognize the lad in uniform, and ever afterward Tom "kept scarce" (in Joe Vardam's terminology) in that vicinity.

In the meantime Tom and Mary often met and in time they came to know each other well. Mary discovered admirable traits in Tom, and

Tom discerned excellent qualities in Mary. Aside from going back to and from school, Tom rarely went out, for he did not know when he might run into Joe Vardam.

Tom was always neatly attired, and presented a pleasing appearance. Wherever he delivered goods for his firm, the people were always satisfied with his service. Some commented upon this, and many an extra dollar he had at the end of the month. He had rented a small room in order to save his money.

To Mary Abbott he spoke but slightly of his past, however great was his yearning to do so. Oftimes he felt that he could trust her with his secret.

Upon Fred Trower's return to the North, he told Grace that he had met a man who informed him that Tom Brinley had been sent to the chain-gang, because he was a thief, an idler, and a dangerous character. But since his description of the man tallied with the appearance of Joe Vardam, Grace would not believe the charges against Tom. She said little to Fred about the matter, however.

Joe Vardam had visited the Grants in the course of his search for Tom. This Grace did not know until after a planned absence, arranged for the purpose of avoiding this man. After she returned, however, she learned that he was in search of Tom Brinley. Then, as if in a vision, she remembered about the woman crying for her lost son,—the black woman of whom the little Grant children had spoken.

Over to the de Forests she went and after speaking to Fanny about the matter, she saw Mandy Brinley and talked with her. After this talk Grace was more than ever convinced of Tom's innocence. For between Fanny and Grace, the conclusion had been established that Joe Vardam was a scheming rascal. So the Grants were kept in ignorance of the whereabouts of Tom's mother. After this visit Grace called frequently to see Fanny, and the friendship between the two grew strong and deep.

CHAPTER XIV

TOM IN LOVE

Time went on and with it Tom had changed, —having grown taller and stouter. Now he had a certain assurance that he could get by better than at first. He was preparing to graduate from Hooper's Institute in his twentieth year, and because of his brilliancy and oratorical ability, he was given the valedictory, which he felt even now unsafe to accept. So, because he begged to be excused, it passed on to the next.

Meanwhile, he had kept up his friendship with Mary Abbott, and though his tender feeling toward her was manifest, he did not dare to speak to her of his love.

"Mary is so hard to read," he would say to himself. "She always seems so sympathetic in her manner, which somewhat puzzles me. She looks at me so tenderly, when she asks me questions regarding my past, and which I try so hard to evade answering. It has been a great task for me to avoid telling her all in the few years in which I have known her. She has been my only comfort through these long and dreary months."

Mary Abbott was preparing to be a domestic science teacher. She worked as maid in a private family during the day, and at night attended Hooper's Institute. Having come from the South, where the advantage for such a training was small, her fondest hope was to go back as a teacher, with this added Northern training, which was so much the envy of the ambitious Southern girl. Tom knew that she would be leaving him the following fall and then he would be left absolutely alone. What would he then do without congenial association? How he longed to keep her with him! If he only dared tell her his secret, and have her help him to find some way out of the awful dread that occasionally overwhelmed him!

"After you have gone from me, Mary, and have taken all that is sweet out of my life, if I could only find my dear mother, to whom I might go for solace! I wonder if she still lives and yearns for her boy! O Mother, what cruel fate has severed us,—who have lived so happily together!"

One evening, at a church social, Mary met her aunt, whom she had not seen since she left the South. It was Nanna, the cook who worked for the de Forest family. Once when Mary was visiting her, she told her aunt of the fine young

TOM IN LOVE

man whom she had met at the Institute and how much he reminded her of Mandy the laundress.

"The eyes are so much alike," Mary would say.

Nanna told her that Mandy was in great distress, as they were seeking the lad who had escaped from the chain-gang and she knew that if they caught him they would lynch him.

"I do feel so sorry for both," said Mary, "for I know they both suffer. It is so sad that those wicked people in the South are not brought to justice."

"Some day them 'white trash' down there will get all they are lookin' for bless the Lord!" returned Nanna.

It was then that Mary began to suspect that Frank Hope was really Tom Brinley,—Mandy's son. And she resolved that at the first opportunity, she would reveal her suspicions to Tom.

One day Tom felt that he must give vent to the pent-up feelings that were getting the better of him. He felt that he must tell some one. In his association at the Institute he came in touch with a number of Catholics. Ofttimes he heard them speak of confession. Then, too, he remembered that one of the boys had committed a theft in a thoughtless moment, and when he thought over what he had done it worried him so much that he confessed to his priest, whose influence went far towards making his punishment a slight one. Then, too, he was rid of the dreadful remorse that attends a hidden crime.

Tom thought over all this very seriously, and determined to go to a priest and tell him his sad story.

"I must unbosom my secret self," he would often say to himself, "for I cannot stand this torture much longer."

Mary Abbott noticed that Tom was greatly worried,—that recently he even evaded her presence.

"If I could only help him, I would be so happy. I am almost sure that he is Mandy's boy. I must tell him that I know it and that I want to help him. His mother would mean so much to him. If I could only bring them together without even Nanna knowing it! How I want to help him! Can he not see that I care enough for him not to expose him?" she reasoned.

That Mary might not consider him rude in his great distress Tom dropped her these lines:

Dear Mary:

Such a spell of melancholy has come over me, because of a great sorrow in my life, that I would not care to burden you with it. When I feel brighter I shall see you.

Yours, etc.,

Frank Hope.

Two weeks passed, during which time Tom was making up his mind just what course to

TOM IN LOVE

take to relieve himself of his great burden. He determined that he would see Father Wesser, to whom he had been referred by a Catholic friend. As he was walking toward the parish, he came face to face with Mary Abbott, who, not having completed her course of studies, was on her way to the Institute.

"Why, Mary," remarked Tom, somewhat surprised, "where are you bound for?"

"I am on my way to school," replied the girl. "And you are out for an evening's walk, I suppose?"

"Not exactly," answered Tom, with a far-away look in his eyes.

"Well, I hope in your melancholia you're not planning to jump into the bay."

"I have had a great sorrow, Mary, which has made me feel quite blue at times; and I was on my way to Father Wesser to confide my troubles in him."

"Confide in me, Frank; I believe that I know your trouble. I have recently surmised it. Do you remember long ago when I handed you that paper that was sent me from the South? Well, from your actions then, from the description, and also from what I have recently heard, I think that you are Tom Brinley."

"O Mary,—don't."

"You will not deny that you are Tom Brinley,—will you?"

"Suppose I do say that I am Tom Brinley; what would you do?"

"What should I do other than sympathize with you,—as I have been doing for the past three years? Now I have a great surprise for you,—one that I wish you to hear of."

Tom looked anxiously into Mary's face.

Mary continued:

"It is your mother that I desire to tell you of. She is laundress in the family with my Aunt Nanna, whom I have only recently found. Now your life I have heard of, as she told Nanna and Nanna in turn told me. You must be very cautious, for the people your mother works for, the de Forests, are great friends of the people whom Joe Vardam stopped with when he was up here searching for you."

Tom's eagerness to see his dear mother knew no bounds. He wanted to go directly to her, no matter what might accrue to him from it, but at the look on Mary's beautiful face when he expressed his rash desire, he yielded to the appeal of her worried countenance and said resignedly:

"All right, Mary. I shall let you arrange a meeting with your own tactfulness. Only let me see my mother as soon as you can."

Mary wondered just how things could be arranged, as Tom's mother seldom went out, and

TOM IN LOVE 105

then only when her Aunt Nanna urged her to do so.

Despite Mary's record for punctuality at the Institute, to-night she felt that she could not leave Tom. Nor did he persuade her to leave him,—though he knew that she disliked to miss her classes,—as he felt that he needed her just then so much. So on they walked and talked, hardly noticing where they were going.

CHAPTER XV

TOM BRINLEY RESCUES GRACE ENNERY

When the young people reached Sixty-ninth Street, they were startled by an alarm of fire. Mary and Tom quickened their steps and hastened to the scene,—in Seventy-first Street.

Volumes of smoke seemed to be pouring forth from the upper windows of a house. A man rushed in and a woman met him at the head of the stairs, pointing above, where they both hastened. Soon he was seen with a child in his arms. He rested her on the step and went up again, bringing down this time a young girl. Neighbors took charge of these. No sooner had the same man gone up again, than flames were seen bursting from the windows. The firemen had not yet arrived, and Tom, forgetting for the moment Mary at his side, ran into the house and up the stairs. He saw that the man was trying to manage a half-dazed boy and a young woman, who was partly overcome by the smoke. Tom, seeing that the man was tottering under the double load, seized the woman and brought her down the staircase. As

TOM BRINLEY RESCUES GRACE 107

he reached the door a neighbor called to him to bring her into the house where the two girls were being cared for.

As soon as Tom reached the air with the woman, she opened her eyes, and looking into the face of her rescuer, cried,

"Why, Tom,—is this Tom Brinley?"

He recognized the woman as one whom he had seen in his Santa Maria home,—Grace Ennery.

"Yes, ma'am," he replied, "but don't expose me, please."

By this time Fred Trower had reached Grace's side with Jack Grant, whom Grace had insisted upon Fred's rescuing, with the rest of the children, before she permitted him to pay any attention to her.

"Fred," she whispered, "this is the boy whom I sent you in search of. He is the one who prevented us from being overcome by the smoke."

Tom put his finger to his lip in order to quiet her, fearing exposure.

"Give your address to Mr. Trower, and we shall arrange to talk with you, Tom. Do not fear anything, as we shall now,—since you have so bravely rescued us,—guard you with our lives."

"Good-by," whispered Tom, as he handed his address to Mr. Trower and hurried out, not wishing to excite attention. To his amazement, he found that as he pushed his way out of the neighbor's house he was confronted by policemen and reporters. In the street there was much excitement, for by this time the engines had arrived and great crowds had congregated. As Tom appeared upon the street, he was greeted with "Bravo! bravo!" from the crowd. Some came up to him and asked his name; but Tom, being entirely unprepared for this notoriety, brushed quickly by the people, refusing to comment upon what he had done.

"Give ye name, ye fool," cried a tough; "ye might git somethin' out er it."

"Don't want anything," answered Tom.

"Then tell us where you live," interrupted a policeman.

"Don't want to," muttered Tom, and pushing by them, he ran up the street.

"Queer guy!" remarked some one in the crowd.

Tom ran home alone in his excitement, leaving Mary waiting for him somewhere in the crowd.

After the fire had subsided and the Grant children and Grace Ennery were permitted to return home, accompanied by Fred Trower, they were temporarily provided for in the lower part of the house. The fire, caused by the short-circuiting of the electric wires, affected

TOM BRINLEY RESCUES GRACE 109

the upper part of the house only, and that part by smoke and water rather than by flames.

When Mr. and Mrs. Grant returned home from a social function, greatly frightened,—as they had been sent for,—the children told them excitedly how a colored man had come to the rescue when Mr. Trower had been almost overcome.

"Who was he, and what was his name?" inquired Mr. and Mrs. Grant, in a breath.

"He wouldn't tell us his name. Did he tell you, Aunt Grace? I saw him talking to you and Mr. Trower," said Jack with much concern.

Grace remained quiet, but Fred Trower broke in:

"He did, but in our excitement we forgot it."

"I thought that I saw him write something down," Margaret put in.

"If he did, I don't really recall it," was Fred's reply.

This conversation was interrupted by the maid, who came in to ask for help in removing some beds to the library. Both Mr. Grant and Fred went out to assist her. After everything had been arranged, Fred left, promising to see Grace on the morrow.

Going directly to the club, Fred remained there talking of the fire and other things until quite a late hour, when he returned home. While undressing for bed, he thought of the exciting events of the evening and of the bravery of Tom Brinley.

"Brave chap!" said Fred aloud, as was his custom in the quiet of his apartment. "I wonder if such a fellow could be a dangerous character. Nevertheless, I'll size him up to-morrow, and will let Grace know what I think of him. Let me see where he lives."

Fred arose, took up his vest and to his great dismay found that the paper was not where he was sure he had placed it. He looked in the other pockets of the clothes that he wore; still he could not find it. His first impulse, of course, was to call up Grace and ask her if she had found the slip of paper that Tom Brinley had given her.

Immediately he went to the 'phone and called up the Grant house. Of course, at this hour of the night, Mr. Grant was the one to answer the call, as all the servants were asleep in another part of the house. A night call always annoyed Silas Grant, as he never cared to be aroused from his sleep. And when both he and his wife were wakened by the ring just outside their door, he remarked:

"Who the devil is calling up at this hour of the night,—after all the excitement, too?"

"I can't imagine," replied his wife. "Prob-

TOM BRINLEY RESCUES GRACE 111

ably some one who has just heard of the fire and is calling up to see if we are all right. Get up, Silas, and see who it is."

Mr. Grant arose reluctantly, and after inquiring who it was and finding out that it was Fred Trower, said:

"What in the thunder do you want to wake us up at this hour of the night for?"

"Awful sorry to bother you, Grant, but I must speak to Miss Ennery upon a matter of very great importance."

"Very great importance, hey? And can't wait until a decent hour to talk to her," snarled Silas Grant. And as he walked through the hall to Miss Ennery's door he muttered: "Wakin' up everybody for a little nonsense."

Grace awoke when Mr. Grant called to her, and impatiently slipping on her boudoir slippers and gown, went to the 'phone.

"Fred, why could you not wait? Mr. Grant does not like this intrusion on his sleep."

"Sorry, Grace, but I could not wait until morning to tell you that I lost the paper with Tom's address on it. Did you find it after I left you?"

"O Fred, how careless of you! What will you do? Something must be done immediately."

"What can I do? I don't know where to find him. I didn't notice what was on the card."

"O Fred, this is dreadful! I'll look around and call you up if I find it. If you don't hear from me, come up to the house before you go to your office and we can determine upon some step to take under these unfortunate circumstances. Good-by for the present."

Grace, depressed, went on a search for the paper which would, however, mean much if found before it fell into another's hand. Joe Vardam had made the name of Tom Brinley well known in the Grant home, as he had stayed with them when he was searching for Tom. As has been said when Grace heard of his coming, she purposely,—without letting the Grants into the secret,—made a visit to a school chum, to avoid identification.

And now the only thing to do was to find the card for should any of the Grants get hold of the paper, it would surely mean a return to the chain-gang for the boy.

Poor Grace searched everywhere for the missing slip of paper, but it failed to materialize. She refrained from inquiring whether or not it had been seen, as she knew that she would surely incur suspicion. Tired and fagged out from the hunt, she returned to her room a most unhappy woman.

Fred called early the next day and they talked seriously of some possible way to save

TOM BRINLEY RESCUES GRACE 113

the boy. They could arrive at nothing definite, and Fred left as quietly as he had entered, promising to think things over and return in the evening.

CHAPTER XVI

SPIRITED AWAY

In the morning's papers much space was devoted to the fire in the Grant household, and there was also a statement to this effect:

A colored youth, whose name could not be ascertained, saved Miss Ennery, the artist (whom reports state will soon marry Banker Trower's son). Fred Trower and Jack Grant were also saved from being overcome. Fred Trower knew at his last going up into the burning apartment that he would have to bring both Miss Ennery and little Jack down, for he was afraid that to leave either would mean sure death to that one. When the colored youth rushed up, he found that Trower's load was too much for him, so, relieving him of Miss Ennery, he enabled Trower to rescue the boy, which was all that he could well do in his overcome condition. Detectives are hunting for the youth, whom the Grants feel should be rewarded.

Grace came down to her breakfast with a careworn look. Mrs. Grant insisted that the girl remain in bed and a physician be summoned; but Grace said she was not ill.

"What is the matter with you then?" inquired Mrs. Grant. "You look positively wretched. You must have attention."

"I thank you, Mrs. Grant, but I must be out to-day; it is important that I should go."

"O Grace, you must not go out; you have had a dreadful shock, and it is telling upon you. Let me do your errand."

"It is so dear of you, Mrs. Grant, but I shall go to bed when I return."

"O Dad," cried Jack, running into the dining-room, all excited, his face very red, "I have found the escaped criminal in my bed!"

Every one was startled and stopped eating to look at Jack. But before any one had a chance to question him, he read aloud:

Tom Brinley, No. 88 —— Street.

The shock was great for Grace, for she had not looked for the exposure in this way. Nevertheless she had presence of mind not to say anything as Jack handed the slip of paper to his father.

"How the devil did this get here?" he asked in a perplexed manner.

"Oh," cried Margaret "that looks like the slip of paper the colored man handed to Mr. Trower,—doesn't it, Aunt Grace?"

"Does it? I was so full of excitement that I did not take notice of what he gave Mr. Trower."

Then excusing herself, Grace hurried to her room, put on her coat and hat, and went out immediately. At the nearest telephone station she called up Fred Trower, arranging for him to meet her immediately. This Fred did in a remarkably short time, and away they went to find the address that Grace bore in mind, for Jack had read it in a very audible manner.

They found the place, but the youth was not at home. Gaining the desired information as to his place of employment, and finding out his assumed name, they called for him at the Bracy establishment.

When Tom heard the news that he was wanted he thought that his hour had come, and as he went into the presence of Fred and Grace, he prepared himself for the inevitable.

They took Tom aside and told him what had happened.

"You must leave immediately, as you are in danger, for these Grants are friends of Vardam's," remarked Grace excitedly.

As if he had been struck with a bolt, Tom recalled the fact that he had delivered a package at this very house, and had come almost face to face with the man who had done him so much wrong.

Grace looked up into her lover's face, saying:

"Suppose, Fred, we send him out of the country? What boats are going out this morning?"

"Let me see—the *Lusanne* sails at twelve o'clock to-day. Do you think he can make it?"

SPIRITED AWAY 117

"Why not?" interposed Grace. "Tom, ask the manager to let you off at our request and we shall see that you get there in time."

Tom obediently did as he was bid, yet in his heart at that moment he was prepared to face the worst.

He was relieved from duty without any trouble, and, giving him money to get suitable clothing for the trip, Grace and Fred left him to meet him again at the *Lusanne's* dock.

As they had a little time, Grace bought for the boy a number of things that she felt he would enjoy having and yet knew he would not get. She had warned him not to return to his stopping place, since she did not know what course Mr. Grant would take.

Grace and Fred were anxiously waiting at the dock when Tom reached there, and having him register as Lester Trower, the name of Fred's dead brother, they supplied him with funds to give him a start at Oxford, where Grace wished him to continue his studies.

Remaining until they saw the boat fairly under way, and with the feeling of security that came of seeing the deep lying between Tom and his enemies, Grace and Fred left the wharf, a happy pair.

"Now, Grace," said Fred, "let us arrange for a quiet wedding in a few days, since your father has given his consent and tells us not to wait for him, as his stay is still indefinite. For a time we can rent an apartment; it's easy enough to make a change when we have found a suitable location. I have a notion that Vardam will be up here in a few days, and I want you to be out of his way. To-day is Wednesday. Let us be married Saturday in the Little Church Around the Corner."

"All right, Fred; perhaps it is the proper thing now. And the coming true of my wish has made me so happy. Yet we never have what we really want, after all, in this life. Things happen so differently from what we desire. I wanted to talk with Tom about his trouble. I firmly believe he met with foul play. Some one wished to do him harm."

"Yes, Grace, I, too, believe in the lad now, since I have seen him and know of his unselfishness. He seems utterly incapable of wrong-doing. His eyes are so wonderfully sympathetic. Poor boy! If he is truly innocent,—as I believe him to be,—his persecutors should be brought to justice."

"Fred, you had better leave me now and return to the office while I go home and rest."

"You need rest surely, for you look so careworn. Go home, and do not worry any more, but get yourself together for the event of our lives,—our wedding."

Grace smiled complacently as they parted,

SPIRITED AWAY 119

Fred going to the office, and she home to rest,—both pleased with the fact that they were able to beat whomever would be first on the boy's trail.

At the dinner-table Grace learned that detectives had already been on the boy's track and that a telegram had been sent to Vardam to acquaint him of the fact.

"I can't see for the life of me," remarked Mr. Grant at the dinner-table, "how that paper could have gotten into my house, unless it was brought in. I shan't rest until I find out the truth."

In the meantime Fred had arranged for a Saturday morning wedding. A dear little apartment, overlooking the Park was the selected spot,—for a while at least.

Fred's father and mother were pleased with the match, for they both knew and respected Banker Ennery's daughter. They had met Grace and liked her, and were very proud of the fact that Fred was attracted toward such a fine girl.

After dinner Grace found Mrs. Grant in her apartment, and told her that she and Fred had decided to be married very quietly the following Saturday, and that she wanted to have her and Mr. Grant present with the children. She also said that Fanny de Forest would be at the ceremony.

"I am glad you are going to marry, Grace," she replied, "but I hope you won't go to work and settle down and never amount to anything socially. Why, even your father went out more frequently than you do."

"That will depend entirely upon Fred, Mrs. Grant. If he cares for society, of course I will adapt myself to his inclinations along this line."

"Oh, he used to go out a good bit, Grace; but since he has been so wrapped up in you, he has not been seen anywhere but at the club."

"Well, I suppose that this and other things will adjust themselves. Nevertheless, what we do socially, and otherwise, I hope will be for the best."

"Saturday morning then, Grace, my dear," remarked Mrs. Grant as Grace arose to go.

When Grace rang the de Forest bell that very afternoon she was pleased to have the door opened by Mandy Brinley. In handing her card to Mandy, Grace said softly:

"Come to this place alone to-night—I must see you regarding Tom."

Mandy bowed understandingly, and hastened to call Miss de Forest, who soon put in her appearance, bedecked like the Queen of Sheba.

"Ah," she cried in her usual spirited manner, "what wind blew you my way to-day, you naughty kid?"

SPIRITED AWAY 121

"I'm marrying on Saturday morning, Fanny, in the Little Church Around the Corner, and I want you present as a witness."

"Sure thing, kid, and I wish you piles of luck. You're getting the real stuff, Grace. Lots of girls have been crazy over him,—got the dough, you know (that is, his dad has, and he the only child). He's some catch, I tell you! Why didn't you have a decent wedding? What's it so quick for? Did the fire drive you to it?"

"No, not exactly," drawled Grace, "and in a way it did. Then, since we were really going to cross the Rubicon, and neither of us cared about a large wedding, we thought we might as well cross now as at any time."

"Well, perhaps you're right. After all, Grace, what's in a wedding? It's the living afterwards that counts in the long run. By the way, they've found Mandy's poor son, haven't they?"

Grace, reddening a bit, replied:

"Yes."

"Mrs. Grant said that they found his card after the fire, and some think he was the lad who rescued you."

"That may be so," said Grace.

"If you could hear his poor mother talk, you would think he was an angel instead of the devil Vardam pictures him to be. Well, I don't know; it's all very mysterious,—that he should be so good and at the same time so bad."

Grace went after Fanny had lavished all sorts of good wishes upon her.

Fanny de Forest was a typical society girl, yet she had a sympathy which Grace thought appealing, and even though Fanny loved to go into society, at every chance she sought Grace and took great delight in her company and in her art. She had a freedom of speech that was attractive in her, though at times she gave it rein until it trampled over the proprieties. Despite this she never, because of her intuitive sympathy, gave offense. Her wholesomeness, combined with this sympathy, had won Grace's friendship.

CHAPTER XVII

THE WEDDING

Saturday morning arrived, and upon this eventful day the Grant household was in great excitement. The children did not feel very happy over losing their Aunt Grace, yet they enjoyed the privilege of attending a wedding.

"Aunt Grace, why can't Mr. Trower come here to live? We'll have room for him after the carpenters get through mending where the fire burned," lisped little Elleen, of whom the household always stood in fear; for no one knew just how frankly she would express her views.

"I shall ask him, Elleen," Grace answered, trying hard to keep back a smile which was forcing its way to the front, while little Elleen, ignorant of the amusement she was causing, continued: "If he doesn't want to go upstairs with Sally and Ann, he can have my bed and I will come in with you."

"You are very, very generous, my dear, and your arrangements will be looked into," Grace replied, while taking her into her arms and fondling her closely.

The day was a wonderfully pretty one in April. The sun shone as perfectly and the air was as balmy as a day in June, and every one seemed in good spirits. Grace was attired in a simple but handsome traveling suit of pearl gray. Business was very pressing and Fred's father did not wish him to leave for any lengthy absence just then, so the bridal pair had planned a short honeymoon trip to Atlantic City.

Mr. Grant returned to the house at eleven-thirty with his chauffeur and all were ready to be taken over to the church.

When the party had reached the church and were about to alight, they noticed some sort of excitement, which seemed unaccountable.

As soon as they had alighted and entered upon the scene, Mr. Grant found that the detectives whom he had engaged to hunt Tom Brinley, had traced Fred Trower as an accomplice to his flight and a warrant had been issued for his arrest.

Everything was in confusion. Fred's father was distracted; Mr. Grant nonplussed.

The detectives then told how Fred and a lady answering the description of Miss Ennery had gone to Tom Brinley's place of abode the morning that the card was found in the Grant home. The detectives had also found out that the boy had been posing under the name of Frank

THE WEDDING 125

Hope, and that he had been in the community several years. He had worked for the Bracy firm, and since he had been North had entered and graduated from Hooper's Institute. They also discovered that, the morning he disappeared, a man and woman, answering to the description of Fred Trower and Miss Ennery had been with him. The three had been traced to the wharf of the *Lusanne,* upon which boat, they learned, the boy had taken passage under the name of Lester Trower.

Grace Ennery and Fred Trower stood speechless during this rehearsal. Both failed to show any emotion, while Mrs. Trower sobbed and Mrs. Grant, between outbursts, stated how terrible it was to bring upon them such disgrace because of a worthless "Nigger."

"Why don't you talk, Fred?" inquired his father.

"I will, Dad, when the time comes. Come on in and let the ceremony go on."

A sadder group never entered a church for a wedding. Mr. Grant remained with the detectives, while the others went forward, where the few witnesses sat.

After the ceremony the Grant children and Mrs. Grant left immediately for their home, while Mr. Grant, the two detectives, Grace, her husband, and Mr. and Mrs. Trower were driven over to the station, where Fred's father arranged matters so that he and his bride could have an unmolested honeymoon.

Fanny de Forest dismissed her own chaffeur, at Mrs. Grant's request, and rode in the car with her and the children, so that they might have an opportunity to talk over the event that had just transpired.

"Well, even if Fred and Grace did spirit the boy away, I don't believe that he was the devil old Vardam said he was," Fanny replied, after a short silence, having learned the facts of the case. Then she went on: "Did they admit doing what they were charged with?"

"No, not one word did either of them utter regarding the affair," returned Mrs. Grant. "Fred Trower said that he would talk when the time came. I don't understand it one bit, Fanny."

"Do you think, since they cannot get the boy, that they will ever take Fred into custody?" asked Fanny, with a serious look.

"Never! Jail Fred Trower for a Nigger? The only inconvenience he would experience would be a long-drawn-out trial perhaps, as it would be interstate. And about all they could do would be to fine Fred for interference with the law."

"Poor Fred,—I believe he is doing it all for her! She is so unprejudiced in her feelings, so loyal! She has a strong flow of anti-slavery

THE WEDDING

blood running through her. Her mother's ancestors, I have been told, came over in the *Mayflower*," remarked Fanny seriously; to which Mrs. Grant hastily replied:

"Yes, but her father and his people were Southern slaveholders. Well, at any rate, it is very mysterious, how they knew him, and how the fatal card was brought into my house."

By this time Fanny's home was reached, and she alighted, promising to see Mrs. Grant and the children soon.

The children, not having understood all that had transpired, sat as quiet as mice all the way, until Fanny alighted, when little Elleen called to her:

"Does the colored woman still cry for her boy who was stolen from her, Aunt Fanny?"

This Fanny pretended not to hear, as she had never mentioned to Mrs. Grant that her laundress was the mother of Tom Brinley. Mandy Brinley, as Fanny knew, was so afraid of Vardam that she wanted him never to know what became of her. Thus she defended Mandy's whereabouts not only from Vardam but also from his friends, the Grants.

When Fanny reached home she was very happy to find Mandy and tell her that her son had escaped to England. She could not account for the fact that Mandy was not as overjoyed as she expected she would be.

"Ain't you glad, Mandy?" asked Fanny.

" 'Deed I is, 'deed I is," replied the poor woman, trying to assume an air of surprise; but the truth was that she met Grace by appointment the very night Grace called at Fanny's home, and had exchanged confidences both regarding the boy and the crookedness of the politics of Santa Maria, which would take advantage of a lad so ambitious as was Tom.

CHAPTER XVIII

THE TRIAL

In spite of the cloud that hung over the heads of Grace and Fred, they spent a delightful honeymoon by the sea. Tom's name was rarely mentioned, for new scenes and new conditions had brought about new thoughts.

While they were away Fred's mother superintended the arrangement of their apartment. Grace's furniture and effects, which were brought from her rooms at the Grants' home, were artistically arranged. The evening they were expected home being chilly and stormy, Mrs. Trower had a cheerful fire made in the grate, and both she and her husband eagerly awaited the arrival of their children.

Supper was waiting when the honeymooners arrived, and they, with the older folks, enjoyed it immensely. Every sad thought seemed far away until Fred's father aroused him to serious thought by asking him how he came to entangle himself with the colored runaway.

Then he and Grace together told the story of Tom Brinley.

"This Joe Vardam is expected on to the trial, which takes place next week," Fred's father informed them.

"Father, I could bring back this lad and turn him over into the hands of these scoundrels, but I won't. Why, his landlady, Hooper's Institute, and the Bracy firm belie every statement to the effect that he is a dangerous character."

The trial was set for the Monday morning after Grace and Fred returned home, but, owing to the fact that Vardam could not be present, it was postponed.

"He can't find any witnesses, I suppose," Fred remarked to Grace the next evening, as they sat at dinner in their apartment.

During the interim Fred gathered all his witnesses, who included all whom the lad had come in touch with since his escape to the North.

Fred was impressed with the fact that they were all eager to appear in behalf of his protégé.

At length Vardam and his witnesses came North, and the day of the trial was set for 10 o'clock of the morning after their arrival.

Mr. Grant, with Vardam, Tilton and their lawyer, were in court and seated long before the appointed time.

Fred, with Grace and their lawyer, made

THE TRIAL

their appearance. Their witnesses included all with whom Tom had been associated since his coming North, also his mother. The courtroom was packed with society folk as well as with those who did not mingle with the upper strata. The unique feature of this case was that wealthy society leaders were defending a Negro runaway at a time when prejudice was so violent.

The judge took his place on the bench and called for order in the court.

He read in measured tones the charge against Fred Trower, who was accused of the abduction of a criminal for whom extradition papers had been made out, and of placing him, under an assumed name, out of the reach of the law.

Then Fred was asked to take the stand. He did so, testifying as to the Grant fire and his meeting Tom there for the first time. He gave a graphic account of the boy's rescue of Miss Ennery and Jack Grant at a time when he, Fred, was almost exhausted, and he told how the coming of this black lad on the scene had prevented all three from being overcome by the smoke.

This news was a shock to Mr. Grant, as he did not for a moment think that Tom Brinley was the rescuer of whom he had heard so much, yet he recovered his poise.

After Fred had finished, Grace was called to the stand. She told of her meeting the lad for the first time in Santa Maria,—an innocent boy, with a desire to be something in the world. She told of the child's love for his Leader, who had died, and of the great prejudice she saw existing between the races. She even went so far as to tell of her conversation with the pursuer of the lad and of what Tom had told her of Vardam. The lawyer on the other side tried to rule out this testimony, but her lawyer showed that it was in order.

Then Tom's landlady was called, and she spoke of the lad's fine qualities and business integrity. The Bracy firm in turn told of the excellent service Tom had given them and how much they appreciated it.

The last witness in Tom's behalf was his mother. She spoke in somewhat broken Southern style, but with earnestness so sincere that it impressed all present to such a degree that one could hear a pin drop during her testimony.

Mandy told of Tom's visit to the Leader's grave, which was constantly kept fresh with flowers. She said that he went over and found the flowers withered the day she last saw him. As he was going he said, "Ma, I'm goin' over to git flowers for de Leader's grave out of the fields of San Joan." She stated that after that she saw him no more.

Tilton and Vardam were very restless in their seats, as they listened to the words that

THE TRIAL 133

their opponents were uttering in behalf of a member of a race that they hated with all their hearts.

Vardam was then called upon, and he arose to his feet. Clearing his throat, he told of every conceivable guilt he could name that the Blacks were associated with. He spoke of black men's assaulting white women, of the Negro's neglect, idleness, and laziness, of their feigning good behavior when the Northern whites were around and of the latter's interference with the Southern laws, making the Negro contemptuous, and hard to manage by his Southern employers.

"May I ask," interrupted the judge, "what this Tom Brinley was sent to the chain-gang for?"

Vardam cleared his throat and replied:

"He was surly, rude, idle, and a dangerous character."

"Did I not hear that he stole?"

"Oh, yes," Vardam quickly responded.

"What did he steal?"

"A number of things."

"Name some of them."

"I object," interposed Vardam's lawyer.

"If I can have one concrete example to place him in the criminal class, I can see where Frederick Trower and his wife protected a criminal. But up to this point, I cannot see where he has been a dangerous character in the community."

"Well, I tell you they are all dangerous,— every confounded one of them."

"That is sufficient," said the judge.

Then Tilton was called to the witness chair.

"What do you know of Tom Brinley," asked the judge.

"Everything bad," answered Tilton, rather glumly.

"What connection did he have with you?"

"He worked for me."

At this remark Mandy Brinley sobbed aloud, for she knew that Tom had never laid eyes upon this man that stood there, lying.

"What work did he do?"

"Worked in my rice-fields, and while there he created disturbances among the other workers."

"Then," remarked the judge, "do I understand that you sent him, for no particular offense, to the chain-gang, where after being driven and lashed and starved, he loosens his chains, steals tools from the drunken guard, beats him into unconsciousness, and escapes? That is what any of us would have done under the circumstances."

At this moment the court-room door opened and Tom Brinley walked slowly down the aisle. Those who knew him could not have been more startled. Tom's mother screamed out, and Joe

THE TRIAL 135

Vardam turned as white as a ghost, as Tom stood there facing the judge.

"Your honor," said he, "I, Tom Brinley, have come back to defend myself."

Vardam, regaining command of himself, caught Tom by the arm and cried:

"You are my prisoner!"

"Order in the court-room," cried the judge. "Release that boy. He is yours only if he is proven guilty." Then, turning to the boy, he asked: "What have you to say, boy?"

The unexpected arrival of the youth,—regarding whom so many conflicting reports had been heard,—was dramatic. He descended upon the court like a bolt from the blue. Every eye was riveted upon him; his face and bearing were closely scrutinized; his manner of speaking, his every gesture was eagerly watched.

And what did the audience in the court-room see? A manly youth of twenty, whose very appearance belied the accusations of Vardam and Tilton. They saw a brown-colored boy, with a broad brow that was crowned with curly black hair; with large, glowing, brown eyes that could flash with indignation or melt with tenderness; with a nose slightly Roman in character; a jaw and chin broad and square; lips firmly compressed, and a face round and full. But the determination that was expressed in that firm mouth and square jaw and chin were relieved from harshness by the twinkle in his eye. And those slightly curved lips could break into a beautiful smile. Not exactly a handsome face, yet it was a decidedly noble one. Suffering and sorrow showed there; but it was suffering and sorrow that had been conquered and mastered that was expressed in that countenance.

And the form they saw was in keeping with the head and face; a form slightly above the medium height, erect, broad-shouldered and deep-chested, with that ease of movement that betokens great strength and agility.

It was easily seen that Tom had made a favorable impression upon his audience before he began to speak in calm, measured tones, with a well-modulated voice.

Amid breathless silence Tom began his story.

He told a most touching tale of his life with his mother at Santa Maria, stating that he did all that he could to help her. He told the court how Vardam laid in wait for him, as was his habit with other ambitious individuals of his race. He told a pitiful tale of the chain-gang, having sufficient presence of mind not to mention Uncle Abbott; yet he did say that he found others there as innocent of crime as he was. He said, in reference to the overseer whom he incapacitated, that he had hoped in his escape to meet no obstacle and that when

THE TRIAL 137

he did meet such in the form of the overseer, that to deal this blow was his only salvation, his only gateway to liberty.

In finishing his story, Tom said that he had an opportunity in his trip to Europe to escape, but when the disabled *Lusanne* stopped off Nova Scotia for repairs,—she having been hurt by storm,—on going ashore he had learned from a New York paper that his benefactors were in trouble because of him. Then he felt that he must return to exonerate these good friends from any blame.

The verdict was written on the faces of the jury as they filed out. While awaiting their return, Tom sat facing the court. He was not conscious of the opinions the people were forming of him; but sat there stoically calm and self-possessed.

CHAPTER XIX

TOM BRINLEY AT OXFORD

Every one in the court-room could not escape some feeling of relief when, after a great suspense, the jury returned with a verdict of "Not Guilty."

For a second everything was silent, and then excitement reigned. It seemed that every one sympathized with Grace and her husband and the lad who had so nobly defended himself.

Tom's mother could not release the boy from her embrace, for her joy at seeing him and knowing that he had his liberty was almost too much for her. All she could utter in her great emotion was:

"My Tom,—Ma's own Tom!"

Vardam and Tilton were absolutely without sympathizers. For every word from Tom's mouth had touched the hearts in the court, as he defended his actions with so much depth of feeling. And even though he was a colored boy trying to prove his innocence, one was moved as he gazed into his deep-set eyes, for in their depths his very soul revealed itself.

TOM BRINLEY AT OXFORD

All said something encouraging to him, and in his simple, unassuming way, he passed out by the side of his mother.

Once outside, Grace urged Tom to go on his trip as soon as his mother felt that she could spare him. This he promised to do. Freed now, he was able to do those things that had been impossible to him before, because of his fear of detection.

What enjoyment Tom took in being able to look the world squarely in the face! The feeling of independence that possessed him could not be expressed in words.

Mr. Silas Grant forsook his Southern friends, for one could see that, apart from the conventional courtesies that he was bound to extend to them, he was eager to be freed of their society.

Silas Grant made it his business to see Tom in a few days and offer to share a portion of his educational expenses. And even after Tom told him that Mr. and Mrs. Trower had amply provided for him, he still proffered his services. Upon his insistence, Tom asked him if he would devote that portion to the comfort of his mother. Mr. Grant said that he was willing to do so, because he felt he must do something for a lad,—even though he was black,—who had been so brave in rescuing one of his children at the time of the fire.

Tom found some time to spend with the companion of his dark days, Mary Abbott. He told her much,—considering the short time he had,—of his feeling for her, and of his desire to make her his wife when he made good. He also told her of her Uncle Abbott, his benefactor, and how he wished that it were in his power to do something for him.

Having attended to all the necessary things,—among them the adopting of his right name in every instance where the name of Frank Hope had been used,—in two weeks' time, in company with his mother and Mary Abbott, Tom stood on the same wharf, again starting after bidding them fond good-bys to carve a destiny for himself in another land.

The steamer *Excelsior,* after an uneventful trip, landed in Liverpool about a week after Tom had embarked. When he reached London he could hardly discern his hand before his face.

"This is one of those dense fogs of which London is famous," he said. "Your welcome is not an enthusiastic one, but, old London, I have faith in you, and in your people, and in your laws."

London was a wonderful city to Tom,—so different from the great metropolis that he had just left. The streets so narrow, the crowds so

TOM BRINLEY AT OXFORD 141

dense, and everywhere people,—great hordes of people.

"The war's killing off of millions does not seem to have produced a scarcity here, at least," remarked Tom to himself.

Everywhere England, the motherland, was in gala attire, because of her great victory. Even though the war had been over some little time, the gay-colored buntings gave evidence of the recent triumphant end of the fight.

This condition of things surprised Tom, for he expected to see nearly every one in mourning, because of the great numbers he had read of who had been slain in battle,—who surely, thought Tom, must have had association with every other person alive.

Tom, in his inexperience, did not realize that this is but the condition that succeeds any great calamity. So quickly are the horrors forgotten that one often wonders with alarm at the indifference to the taking of human life.

Tom was greatly impressed with the treatment he received in this great city. Deference and respect lined his pathway. Nowhere was he made to feel that he was different from any one else. As he wrote to Mary Abbott:

I feel so different here. There is no prejudice anywhere. My color appears to be only an accident, as does the color of one's hair or eyes. I may exaggerate conditions, Mary, but it seems as if the English people are extremely courteous because I am colored,—their desire seeming to be to make me disregard the fact that I am different from other people. I feel that I should like to remain here and never come back to my country, where I am spurned and treated as though I were responsible for that for which God alone is accountable.

Tom established himself with a very pleasant English family, all the members of which were extremely kind to him; and after a few days he gained admittance to the great English University, Oxford.

He was delighted with this old English institution, from which had sprung some of the greatest scholars the world has ever known. Every instructor was keen, earnest, and sincere. Every student had an equal chance. The great war affected this institution very little, for within its walls all races and nations were represented. As time went on, Tom met many interesting characters,—among them, some Africans, who were enrolled there. There was one Siami,—a brilliant Negro, black as the Ace of Spades, but as rich as Crœsus; his father was king of a tribe in his native land, and the vast territory upon which he lived was rich in gold mines. Of him Tom wrote home:

He mingles with royalty and has advantages over the white man without a title, for he is admitted into inner royal circles, and upon festive occasions he takes precedence of those who are below a king in rank.

Tom's letters were always interesting, and Mrs. Trower, Mary Abbott, and his mother

TOM BRINLEY AT OXFORD 143

were his constant correspondents. As for Grace Trower, she was enthusiastic over Tom's letters, and the zeal with which the boy took up his work.

Westminster Abbey, wherein are buried all the English celebrities, was the place in which Tom loved to wander. For hours he would sit and study this last resting-place of England's famed sons, awed and impressed by its silent grandeur.

Mary Abbott kept Tom in touch with his country's activities. After he was away two years, great excitement was being manifested over the country's threatened war with Japan. Then, too, the question that his people were pressing was "The admittance of the Negro into the State Militia." "No," cried many; "Yes," cried a few. "What are we," exclaimed Tom, on reading of the issue, "that even to die for one's country is too great an honor?"

Tom, on account of his excellent record, was admitted into some of the most exclusive societies of the University. He was even privileged to attend social functions. The social attitude of the English people puzzled him, for he thought that socially his color would be a barrier as long as he lived, so far as mingling with white man was concerned. Though enjoying every privilege, Tom never took advantage of this liberty given him, and he seldom entered into the social life that he was so often urged to share.

Mrs. Trower did not stint Tom at all in the matter of allowance. She was eager for him to imbibe all he could from educational sources. She encouraged him to visit historic places throughout Europe. Although the war had left its mark of devastation to a greater or less degree on the different countries, she felt, nevertheless, that he could picture in his imagination what it had been.

It was interesting to Tom to watch the women in the different avenues of work, which before had been filled by men. Outside of England women predominated. Everywhere he went Tom was forced to the conclusion that she could never be denied the ballot for which she had fought so arduously. He found, however, upon investigation, that in nearly every country that had participated in the war the women had been permitted to vote. Only England was still orthodox in this particular, and her Pankhursts were still knocking at the door of Parliament and the House of Commons, but without success, even though much progress had been made by the feminists.

"Why is it," asked Tom of an English friend, "that the women are so persistent and rash

TOM BRINLEY AT OXFORD 145

in their demands?" For they still made raids upon assembled political bodies.

Felton, the Englishman to whom he had put the question, answered:

"We English do not comply with the requests of our women, without forethought. We do not believe that it is good for women to have what we have decided is not good for them. Our attitude towards our women is the same as the Southern attitude is towards your people. We believe that women should always be subservient to men, and to place the ballot in their hands would surely make them the equal of men; and that we Englishmen do not wish."

Whereupon Tom inquired:

"How is it that the countries all about have granted her this privilege?"

"So many would not have done so, if it had not been for the war, which, taking so many of their men, necessarily made the countries, to a great degree, dependent upon their women," was the reply.

Tom had many leisure hours while in England, and in them he often thought of his dear ones so far from him, and of his beloved Leader's grave. His greatest sorrow was the fact that he never could feel safe to return to his own home town and visit this spot, which he knew had been long neglected.

"How long," he would ask in his sorrowful

mood, "will Vardam and Tilton hold their cruel sway because of politics?"

Not many days after one of his periods of thinking of Santa Maria he received a letter from Mary, who was then teaching in a Southern school. In it she sent a newspaper clipping, which read as follows:

The Vance Institute has closed its doors. So indifferent were its students to what the great John Vance saw fit to leave for an unworthy people that it could not continue to open its doors to emptiness.

In the letter Mary stated that politics had grown so rotten in and around Santa Maria that the appropriation left in trust had been misused, and that there were no funds left to keep this greatest of Southern Institutes open to the people that it was intended to help. Then she added:

If some one could have followed the Leader, who, like him, had the love of his people at heart, things would not have taken the course that they did.

"Following the Leader," breathed Tom. "Could I but do this, Mary, it would be the realization of my dearest wish. But I cannot follow the Leader in Santa Maria. If I follow him, it must be elsewhere."

Time passed and Tom made many good friends. He applied himself arduously to his studies, never feeling that he could spend any time for those things that did not tend to advance him along the road toward the responsibility that Mrs. Trower had made his goal.

Mary still continued to keep Tom in touch with American affairs. Her letters were a great source of delight to the student, because they were so full of cheer and encouragement. And there were times in Tom's life as well as in the life of other ambitious individuals, when the worker needed a cheering word from home, for they served as stimulants along life's rugged paths.

Tom's mother was still with the de Forests, who were extremely good to her. Often she wrote to Tom that the Grant children kept her cheerful, and that Mrs. Grant constantly looked after her wants. Grace Trower always inquired after Mandy when she went to see Fanny, who had become her very dear friend.

"Grace kid," Fanny would say, in her usual buoyant manner, "you are the real dope. I want you always to be where I can get to you easy, if I'm in bad. You'll always fix me up. You know what you're up to every time, kid, and that's more than a lot o' them know."

Four years had passed since Tom set sail for England, and time had wrought many changes. Margaret Grant was a young woman, out of school, and ready to be launched into the world of fashion by a society-loving mamma, and to

148   HOPE'S HIGHWAY

be kept upon this social sea by a rich papa. Jack, whom Tom Brinley helped Fred Trower to rescue from the fire, was off to Yale, shining, as most Jacks do, in the athletic field. Elleen did not sing "Eeny, Meeny, Miney Mo" now, but had stolen over to Fanny's and hunted Mandy, to whom she had become much attached. And the greatest of all changes was that Silas Grant had become a director of the Negro Protective Federation.

And in the Trower household noteworthy changes had taken place too. Here you will find a baby girl of three prattling around in merriest glee. She has made the Trower happiness complete, and Grandpa Ennery gets a generous portion of happiness under the spell of Baby Edythe's winsome smiles. And this little one knows Tom Brinley, because of her mother's talks of him, especially at this time, when in her home much is being said concerning the advisibility of Tom's return.

CHAPTER XX

THE CALL OF HIS PEOPLE

The Trowers showed great interest in Tom Brinley's letters. The unprejudiced condition abroad appealed to them particularly, and for that reason they were convinced that Tom, having completed his Oxford course, could not do more wisely than cast his lot under England's skies.

As for Tom, he was eager to return, but he could not decide what to do.

"The North does not need me; her colleges and universities are open to the Negro, but positions are closed to him; therefore, there is nothing for me to do there," he thought.

The Negro Protective Federation had its quota of Negro men employed, he learned on inquiry, yet the many advantages offered Tom in England compensated in a measure for his disappointment. They did not wholly satisfy him, however. He wanted to see his mother and Mary, whom he had not grown to care for one whit less.

Grace Trower was eager to see what Oxford

had done for Tom, and hoped that he might venture to return and engage in active life in the South; but she became thoroughly convinced that such a move would be foolish on his part, when a paper from Santa Maria was sent to Mr. Grant, and he in turn sent it over to her. This paper stated that if Tom Brinley, the Negro ex-convict, ever planted foot upon land below the Mason and Dixon line,—while the present political party was in power,—he would again be immediately seized and put into the chain-gang, where he and his whole race belonged.

"That is dreadful!" cried Grace, after she had read the extract to her husband.

"Dweadful! dweadful!" lisped little Edythe, who, apparently, took it all in.

"We had better send him this paper and advise him to remain on the other side until things look more favorable over here. He, no doubt, will very easily find something to do."

Tom, on receipt of the information, decided that his lot must be cast in Europe.

"When I get money enough I shall send for Mary and marry her; and we will spend the rest of our lives over here," he mused.

Having developed into a powerfully built man by this time, Tom was devoted to athletics, and because of his prowess had gained much honor at Oxford.

THE CALL OF HIS PEOPLE 151

On the completion of his course at the University a position was offered him in the newspaper world. *The London Times,*—being a daily paper of large circulation, paying its employees well,—gave Tom an excellent field for his talents, as well as affording him an opportunity to travel.

France and Germany, it appears, had never settled a disagreement over some African land, and Germany threatened to fight France in order to make her withdraw her claim to this territory. At this time, Tom visited France in the interest of his paper and found that that country was calling for recruits. So impressed was he with the attitude the Frenchmen held towards the Negro soldier,—against whom no discrimination was shown,—that he decided to return to England, resign from his paper temporarily, and enter the French army. Tom had been drilled in military tactics at Oxford, and had hoped for a chance to serve his own country by entering the service at home, if it were possible. His visit to France opened his eyes to the fact that all men were equal in the French army, and his joy at this discovery knew no bounds.

So, into the army he went; promotion quickly followed, till at length, as commander of a regiment, he led a successful charge upon the enemy, sweeping them from their position.

This was a charge that had much to do with the settlement of the question at issue. The territory became the property of the French.

Commander Brinley's fame now resounded through France, and England caught up the strain,—for was it not because of her training that Tom had served so well? Medals of honor were bestowed upon the Negro and he was lauded to an enviable degree.

Tom's mother received from him a letter, in which he told her that he would join the French army and fight, since he could not fulfill his greatest desire,—the serving of his people in his native land. But he added:

"I am serving my people just the same, Mother, by doing something that gives me an opportunity of acting a man's part."

Mrs. Trower did not think so kindly of Tom's adventure, for she felt that if he were to die in battle, every hope that she had fostered for him would be entirely destroyed. When she read of his great achievements, however, her husband remarked:

"Grace, unless you should see the gratitude of France to her warriors you couldn't understand it. It is marvelous how they are lauded. The French worship their heroes as if they were gods."

Tom's chance for making money both in

England and France was now excellent. He received many letters offering him such positions as would have flattered the vanity of many an ambitious youth. This *enbareas de choix* was confusing. Tom was trying to decide just where he would settle and into just which of the open avenues he would turn,—governing his choice always by what he considered would be most agreeable to Mary, whose prayers had followed him in and out of battle,—when he wrote to her that, as soon as he could settle upon one of the many advantageous offers held out to him, she must cross the ocean, and become his wife, according to her promise.

No sooner had he sent his letter off to America than he received a Santa Maria newspaper of recent date, marked with a great cross in ink at the head of a column that read as follows:

GREAT DEMOCRATIC RING OF SANTA MARIA BROKEN—VARDAM'S AND TILTON'S POWER KILLED—REPUBLICAN RULE THE RESULT OF THE RECENT ELECTION—VARDAM AND HIS GANG HAVE BEEN ACCUSED OF GRAFT—MISAPPROPRIATION OF MUCH OF THE STATE'S MONEY.

Then, too, in the text occurred this passage:

After investigation, it was found that through their dishonest maneuvering, the Vance Institute,—that heavily-endowed school for which Enoch Vance so arduously toiled,—had lost everything, and its doors were closed because of the deficit. Who is there to follow that grand and noble leader and once more place upon a solid footing this institute, the pride of the South?

Tom closed the paper, laid it down, and, with his face buried in his palms, he pondered. At this moment there came a knock at the door. He occupied a suite in one of the finest French hotels. The *garçon,* speaking in French,—which Tom understood well,—told him that he was wanted below. Rising, he descended a magnificent stairway and entered a luxuriously appointed salon, where a representative of the President of France awaited him. Tom's visitor informed him that he was authorized to offer him an important consulate.

When Tom had expressed his appreciation of the conference of this great honor upon him, —he said quietly:

"Duty calls me across the seas to my oppressed and forsaken people. I must go and serve them; I must spend my days in lifting them out of their igorance, so that their condition may be altered. I thank you for the great opportunity you have given me to prove my manhood. To England I owe much, because of the advantages she gave me of an education without restrictions. I shall go to my people, taking those European ideals, which I trust shall ever be a part of me, and my prayer to the Almighty shall be for strength to bear un-

THE CALL OF HIS PEOPLE 155

complainingly the scourge of prejudice, which, because of unfair laws, has been allowed to run wild in my own, my native land.''

In a few days Tom was *en route* to America.

As he leaned over the rail to bid good-by to England and France,—secure in the strength of the glories of centuries,—and afterwards turning his face toward his own land, he said:

"I come back to you, my country, which I love and revere. You have unjust laws; you are unfair to my people; but I believe in your future. I have faith in you, though you mete out partial justice to me and mine, and I shall believe in you as long as I hear Christ's name among you. For through Supreme Love only may I and my people hope for a greater freedom.''

Tom's coming was a surprise to all. And the joy of the Trowers, especially Grace, could not be imagined. They, with the Grants, had hoped that he would find some worthy occupation in Europe; but when they were told of what had occurred in Santa Maria, and of how he was on his way to offer his services to the Vance Institute, with the aim of devoting the rest of his life to the carrying out of the glorious work that the great Leader had started, they could not understand how he could turn his back upon a career rich in honors, in order to serve a hopeless institution.

But without one thought of reward, Tom went where duty beckoned. His mother went with him,—happy to look upon old scenes once more.

As the years went on Tom, with Mary his wife, kept up their zealous efforts in the interest of their people in Santa Maria.

Did he raise Vance Institute to its former glory? Yes, nor was that glory all. He did more; for never again in the history of Santa Maria do we hear of the injustice of the Whites to the blacks—never again did a Brinley, or an Abbott, or any other member of the Negro race, know the ignominy of working in the chain-gang. For Tom Brinley had turned his people's steps away from the rough road of ignorance into the happy highway of hope.